postcards *from a* dead girl

HARPER ● PERENNIAL

NEW YORK ● LONDON ● TORONTO ● SYDNEY ● NEW DELHI ● AUCKLAND

postcards

from a

dead girl

A Novel

Kirk Farber

HARPER ⬤ PERENNIAL

HarperCollins books may be purchased for educational, business,
or sales promotional use. For information please write:
Special Markets Department, HarperCollins Publishers,
10 East 53rd Street, New York, NY 10022.

FIRST EDITION

Designed by Jennifer Daddio / Bookmark Design & Media Inc.

Library of Congress Cataloging-in-Publication
Data is available upon request.

ISBN 978-0-06-183447-9

10 11 12 13 14   OV/RRD   10 9 8 7 6 5 4 3 2 1

for
kelly

The postcard is everything, but looks like nothing. An inconsequential sheet of pressed pulp decorated with a few drops of ink, it barely exists in the physical realm. But this one has got hold of something inside me that feels like forever. I follow the looping lines that make up Zoe's penmanship, the soaring arcs and inky swirls. I try to understand the true implications of her words, the hidden message behind the surface one. What a ridiculous phrase: wish you were here.

My throat starts to burn because I'm getting upset. My head feels hollow. Tiny white spots float in my field of vision. I know this means that the lilac thing is about to happen again, and sure enough, it follows like always—a sweet scent floating through the room, a palpable sense of time blurring. My vision and movement go syrupy in a moment of wooziness, as if the universe has slowed everything down so I'll pay attention. But my hearing remains crystal-clear.

I'm sitting on my living room couch, so what I hear is the TV—*Messages from the Other Side*, I think is the show. John the TV psychic says someone is coming through, an old woman named Wilkins, and she needs to talk to a J name. He follows with specific facts: Grandma Wilkins liked to make pasta in the kitchen and spread it out all over the house to dry; she was a closet smoker; on her left breast she had a rose tattoo that her high school boyfriend had convinced her to get.

Nobody else could have possibly known these things.

The family member in the audience, her heart clenched, nods and cries, then can't hold it back anymore and yells out, "Yes! That's Grandma Rose!" in such a genuine outpouring of grief and hope and joy and hurt that it's all too clear she is not an actress, and this is not a feigned reality TV show. Somehow, inexplicably, this is the real deal.

So sincere is her reaction that I realize I'm crying too, and it's caught me off guard. I mean, I don't even know Grandma Rose. And the damn lilac scent keeps tickling my nose and I can't stop the tears even if I want to, and I don't.

Then it stops. Time returns to its normal pace and the smell is gone. A commercial for macaroni and cheese flickers on TV. I feel dizzy and anxious, like I've just missed something. I wait for more, but the weird moment is gone.

My fingertips vice-grip Zoe's latest postcard. This one's supposedly from Barcelona. "Dear Sid, I'm having a wonderful time!" it says in frilly writing. And underneath those words, that awful cliché: "Wish you were here!"

"Wish I was where?" I ask the postcard. "Where the hell are you?" I whip the card across the room, Frisbee-style, but it tips up, does a loop, and floats unharmed to the ground.

John the TV psychic returns to relay communications of forgiveness and healing to the family member in the audience, who has now recovered from her crying spell. I'm not crying anymore either, but I'm not feeling consoled. I'm wishing that just once the psychic would make contact with a malevolent spirit who is still pissed at the living, who has only messages of doom and foreboding.

That's what I feel like lately, a spirit. I find myself staring at the walls a lot, like a zombie. I know I'm doing it, but there doesn't seem to be a proper alternative. When I'm not staring, I'm throwing things. I'm a thrower. Coffee cups. Chairs. Inanimate objects that may have wronged me. Things that get in my way.

My mother was a kicker. If the cat got in her way, she would kick it out of the way. I caught her once, doing this kicking, and stared at her, horror-stricken. "I didn't kick it," she pointed out. "I moved it." I guess that made Mom a mover. I'm a thrower.

I call my sister, Natalie, and tell her about my experience. She's a physician. I don't tell her everything. I tell her I think I'm catching a cold and that my head slowed down, got kind of gummy.

"Sounds like fever symptoms. I wouldn't worry about it, Sid," she says.

"You're sure."

"Get more sleep, drink more fluids, ride it out."

There's something else, I tell her.

"Besides the fever?"

"Yeah. I sort of smelled something."

"What do you mean?"

"It was sort of flowery." I deliberately choose not to mention that it was lilac. "It was really strong, then gone."

This makes her pause.

"What?" I ask. She should know by now not to be quiet for too long when I'm waiting for a diagnosis.

"Has this happened often?"

"Once or twice."

She makes a clicking noise with her tongue. "It might be good to

get you in for a CAT scan, Sid. Sudden, strong smells can be associ-
ated with brain problems. Not to scare you, but just to be safe."

"You mean like tumors?"

"Not necessarily."

"You think I have a tumor."

"I didn't say that."

"I'm the walking dead is what you're saying."

"Forget the CAT scan. Just call me if it happens again."

"A zombie," I say under my breath.

"You're fine, Sid. Probably just a fever."

We say our good-byes. Natalie jokes that I'm a hypochon-
driac, but she's been less patient with me lately as she's expecting a baby and the first trimester kicked her in the ass. I guess
she can comfort only so many needy souls. Ever since Mom and
Dad died, she's played an unspoken parent role, but with her own
little parasite slowly sucking the life force out of her, she doesn't
need me calling so often.

If I ever told her that Zoe was sending me a steady stream of
postcards from the other side, I'm sure she would have me committed.

chapter

3

Gerald the Post Office Guy is an affable
man. He's patient and articulate and well-
groomed, and has no interest in anything
about anyone's life other than package type and
rate of delivery. In short, he's a professional. A postmaster who
doesn't have time for dithering. That's why I'm huddled outside
in my car, memorizing every detail of each postcard, preparing
myself with a matched professionalism for his inevitable questions. I don't want to be like the rest of the nervous customers.
I brought the whole stack with me today to get a reasonable explanation.

Through the post office's plate-glass windows I see that traffic
is finally waning; I will now have a captive audience in Gerald. I
make my way up the steps, through the revolving doors, and line
my toes up on the red line.

Gerald sorts envelopes with purposeful hands, stamps at
them with a large square block. Then he tosses them into a bin
and nods curtly to himself. Finally, he looks up at me. "How can I
help you today?" So nice and orderly. So perfect.

I pour the postcards out on the counter. I forget everything
I'd rehearsed. My mouth falls open a little and I stare straight

through Gerald's ashen face, his pale blue eyes, his silver hair. He looks dead.

"Sir?" he asks.

"Yes," I say, and come back to the living. "I received these in the mail recently and I was wondering if you could explain something to me." I hand him the one from Spain that reads "Fun in the Sun."

Gerald looks the mail over with a careful eye, intrigued by the mystery I've laid out before him. "You say you received these recently?"

"Right," I say, and spread the cards out like a tarot deck. Tulips from Amsterdam. Bier Gartens from Germany. The Eiffel Tower. Big Ben. The Roman Coliseum.

Gerald picks one up, checks my address, then looks at me carefully, like he recognizes me from somewhere else.

"What?" I ask.

"These are all postmarked a year ago," he says.

"Exactly."

"Did you get them all at once?"

"No, they come every few days."

Gerald's face broadens with amusement, like he's found a caterpillar crawling across his desk. "There must have been a glitch in the European system that stopped the mail. Maybe they got lost and found again. It's not uncommon for postcards to get the least amount of attention."

"Do you think it would happen in all these different countries?"

Gerald purses his lips. "That is awfully strange. All I know is the USPS wouldn't be responsible for this. We have strict laws on changing postal dates. Some folks try to send things twice with the same postage. We call it 'skip.' " He makes direct eye contact with me. "Skip is illegal," he says.

"Is there any way to find out where these are coming from?"

"You could check the international codes where they originated." He points at the numbers in the stamp marks. "But chances are you won't find an individual responsible."

I gather up the cards.

"Sorry I couldn't be of more help," he says.

I nod.

"You don't have any packages to send?"

I give my head a solemn shake. Gerald appears genuinely disappointed.

"Let me know if there's anything else I can do for you."

"Thanks," I say and start to walk out, ready to throw something.

"You know," Gerald calls after me, "there's one more option."

I freeze, and turn.

"Maybe the sender is playing a trick on you. It's not uncommon for mail fraud activity to be of a juvenile nature, as serious as it is." Gerald points up to the FBI posters on the wall, to the faces of serious men with serious facial hair, rough pencil sketches of hardened mail-fraud criminals.

"Thanks," I yell back, "but they're from a woman."

"Well—"

"And she's dead, I think."

Gerald leans his head back and looks around the room. "That's a pretty good trick."

"Yeah," I say, and push the glass door open, wishing I could throw it a thousand yards.

Zoe was needy. She needed to be entertained and she needed to be the center of attention all at once. She liked verbal descriptions of my love for her. She wanted to hear them every day, and preferred them to be wildly original. Not "I love you this much," or "I love you tons." It had to be unique, and she wanted specifics. At first I was unskilled at this. I would say things like "I have oceans of love for you."

"Really?" she would ask, and act surprised and flattered, then follow it immediately with "How much do you *really* love me, Sid?" This was my cue to get more creative. I eventually found myself getting quite crafty, and soon I realized this game was not so much about her need to be told she was loved as it was her personal test to measure her mate's spontaneity and intelligence. We'd been inseparable for weeks, Zoe and I, making love several times a day, which was always so intense and blinding and followed by that deep blue bliss. Such a drug, Zoe was.

"If I ever owned my own pharmaceutical company," I told her once, as we stared at the ceiling in her bedroom, "I would put this feeling into a turquoise capsule and call it Blue Zoe Bliss. It would be more popular than aspirin and would soon be followed by world peace. That's how much love I'm feeling right now." She was impressed with that one, and I realized that my metaphors for love had little to do with my spontaneity and intelligence and more to do with the deep love I was feeling for this girl. I was addicted to her. Addicted to Zoe.

Once we took a trip to New York City. Every morning we would walk hand in hand through Chinatown. Zoe liked to listen to the different Asian dialects barking back and forth through the market. We'd make our way to Little Italy and have an espresso at a café, and inevitably Zoe would stare into the black liquid of her cup and try to imitate the Chinatown market workers. "Ning maa," she said, quietly and with great contemplation, both of us knowing she can't speak a word of Mandarin or Cantonese. "Bee naw noo."

"There's this building on 50th and Sixth Avenue," I responded, "and if it were a completely empty husk with airtight walls, it could hold 7,400,000 cubic feet of fluid. If my love were water, this building would be overflowing. The flood damage would result in forty million dollars of repairs."

"Ning maa," she cooed and smiled at me. "Ning maa-aah."

"How would you like to be making double what you're making now?"

This is the voice embedded in my ear. It's my boss, Steve. Steve has omniscient control over the headsets. He can click in at any time to monitor sales conversations, and often delights in offering us dazzling motivation—like asking us if we want to double our income. At times his voice is unexpected and it seems as though it's coming from God, if God were an arrogant salesman drowning in self-delusion.

"I'm telling you, Sid, you could easily be making fifty, sixty grand right now if you were more committed." He claps as he talks, to emphasize the immediacy of my potential income. "Do you want that? Do you really want it? Because it's time to take names and bring in the beaucoup bucks, buddy."

"Sounds great, Steve," I mutter to myself. The reality is that nobody in this entire room of cramped cubicles makes anywhere close to Steve's ambitions, and everybody knows it. I think Steve knows it too, but sometimes I wonder. He's been promising us bonuses for months now and they always seem to be just around the corner.

To keep up hope, my cubicle walls are plastered with vacation posters: couples walking on sandy beaches in exotic locations, families frolicking in theme parks, adventure travelers parachuting and kayaking and snowboarding. The coverage is so complete it's like wallpaper. Everywhere I look, people are having amazing times, living large on my five-foot-by-seven-foot cubicle walls.

The work week goes by in order of the packages we sell. Mondays and Tuesdays are standard vacation packages, #1–15. Europe mostly, escorted group tours through countries like England, France, and Germany. Nothing terribly original. These are the bulk packages sold to the masses: families, retirees, empty-nesters, senior citizens— people who need more guidance through foreign lands. Eight days and seven nights to Rome and Florence. Five nights in beautiful, romantic Paris. Ride a double-decker bus through London and see the queen. Shit like that.

The hardest calls come in the beginning of the week. Mondays are always full of people conferring with their spouses or live-in parents while I wait on the phone. A lot of people refer to me as The Man on the Phone. As in, The Man on the Phone says we should see the canals of Venice. Or, The Man on the Phone says we can't call back, it's a one-time offer. And in the background, grumpy old men who are wondering how their Social Security checks will cover it all say: Tell him to stop calling. Tell The Man on the Phone to fuck off. But I'm used to it. To them, I'm not really a man in the human sense. I'm just a sound wave traveling through lines of fiber-optic cable.

Wednesdays and Thursdays we sell Caribbean cruises and last-minute getaways. These are easier days because people of all ages like cruises, although I don't know why anyone would want to be trapped on a giant boat with three thousand other people for days on end. These customers, though, are nicer, maybe because they're thinking of sun and sea and surf, and anyone offering this potential can't be all bad. Maybe that's what they're thinking. Generally their pause for consideration is longer, and I get to chatting up the package, which is a little more work, but I like the idea of putting pictures in people's heads—creating false realities that they're surely embellishing more than I ever could. Plus, like I said, they're nicer. Sometimes they even sincerely apologize that they can't take me up on my offer. Often on these days I'm not referred to as The Man on the Phone interrupting dinner, but the invisible Bringer of Gifts. And when the inevitable conference with the spouse happens, it's like this: There's a *package available* for a cruise to the Bahamas, or, *there's a deal going*. It's about the deal, not the man bringing the deal. These are the days I wish they could call me back because I bet they would. But that's against company policy, and there's really no way to call back, due to the phone system. The Randomizer, we call it.

Friday is the wild-card day. A hundred percent commission. Eco-trips, Galapagos Islands, Kenyan safaris, you name it. We work with other vendors and sell as big as we want. Fire and Ice trips to Iceland, Bananas and Botflies in Belize. It's sort of like being a Kia salesman who's allowed to sell Porsches for a day. It can feel like a Mexican market; people actually haggle for better prices. Occasionally I take them up on it. And some days, like today, I stare at the posters in my cubicle and imagine myself somewhere else.

This afternoon, I do something I haven't done in a long time. I call Zoe's old number. I override The Randomizer and do a direct-dial, which is strictly forbidden. The pattern of her number makes an incomplete circle. It rings once. I hang up immediately.

The next day is like the day before. Phones ring. Numbers flash on my monitor. I'm tempted to bypass The Randomizer again, but Steve is roaming through the cubicle farm today, lurking around corners, waiting to pounce with his infusion of motivation. It's unsettling.

As crazy as Steve is, he has one redeeming quality: he allows us to work our own hours. We can come in at noon if we want. Or skip a day. As long as we hit our sales mark, he's not worried about how long it takes. He prides himself on being a sort of guerrilla sales manager that way. I don't often hit my weekly minimum, but I get as close as some other losers here. He also gives us employee discounts on vacation packages. So he's not a bad guy.

That being said, I really shouldn't manipulate the phone system. This upsets him greatly, and he can get excitable. He's not all together, I think. He has a tendency to get overzealous. He wears his shirt collar too tight, which seems to cut off the blood supply to his head, often resulting in a beet-colored face, which is the opposite of what you think would happen. And then there's all that clapping.

The best example of Steve's nature is simply the name he

created for the company: Wanderlust Incorporated. It's a clever name, but if customers aren't familiar with the term and they hear me say, "Hi, this is Sid from Wanderlust, calling to tell you about an exciting offer," they hear *lust* and *exciting* together and hang up. Either that, or they talk dirty, and we've been instructed to keep the sell "hot," or keep it going, even through the dirty talk. This was something Steve found ingenious about the name, its supposed subliminal effect on customers. He's sure it has a psychological impact on sales. This is another reason I don't think he's all together.

I was finishing a call last week, wrapping up the credit card information with a quiet older woman who'd just bought a seven-day Ireland bus tour for her and her husband of fifty years. And Steve piped into my ear, whispering, almost seductively, about the beauty of the moment. "You got her, man," he said softly. "She is yours. You own her. This is the beginning, buddy. Start taking names."

The trick is not talking back to the voice. On more than one occasion I've almost talked to the Great Steve in the Sky. More than once I wanted to say: stop talking already about the massive increase of incomes and dreams coming true, and quit it with the promise of bonuses and getting a fat slice of the pie. It's pathetic, this sales rhetoric, and I pity you for having such passion for selling. They're vacation packages, for God's sake.

Perhaps even more pathetic is how I secretly wish all of his bullshit would come true, even though I know all the loud clapping in the world can't do that kind of magic.

"The Randomizer is down, everybody," Steve's voice says in my head, and dozens of other heads behind dozens of other cubicle walls. "Read the numbers off the monitors and go manual!" He claps and it feeds back in my ear. "Hey Sid," Steve says a little quieter, and chucks me in the shoulder. I didn't realize he was that close by. And I don't think he knows his own strength. "You get your blog done yet?"

"Blog?" I ask carefully, and turn to see Steve standing right next to me, his face twisted up in confusion, as if I'd just spoken Swahili. It seems the postcards have been mutating my insides and affecting my ability to interact with other humans. People are slow to understand me, and I'm having more and more difficulty making sense of their conversations, or, more correctly, why they are even having them in the first place.

"I sent the e-mail a week ago," he says. "Everybody writes a monthly travel blog."

"What are we supposed to write about?"

"Anything that will induce sales, help customers feel better about travel in another country. Why don't you write . . ." He spreads his hands out, like he's showing off a marquee. "Pain in the Summer Sun," he says.

I scribble notes. "How many words?"

"Two or three hundred is plenty. It's a blog. Keep it short."

"Do you think that's a good idea?"

"Excuse me?"

"Writing about pain? Is that really going to induce sales?"

Steve frowns at me. "Come on, Sid. What's the matter with you? Sss-pain," he hisses. He walks away, then yells back over the cubicle walls, "Spain, Sid, Spain!"

I wait until he's out of sight, and then I do it again, dial the incomplete circle. It rings, and rings. My heart jumps. Another ring. I realize I'm holding my breath. I wonder if this phone might never be answered. It goes on ringing. I stare at the list of numbers on the monitor.

The phone ringing becomes a mantra, a background noise. My heart plays a clave beat over the bass line repetition. My eyes glaze over. The cubicle goes blurry. I stare through the blue of the monitor and see a perfect, vacation-poster ocean. I am swimming through pure blue, flying through it, weightless, free. Polaroid pictures float past me, the ones Zoe took and then knife-scraped sunrays beaming from our heads. She appears now and tosses more pictures, laughing, shaking her head at me. She's got a phone trapped in the crook of her neck, her shoulder pushing into her ear. "What are you doing?" she asks. "Don't you want this?"

I'm spellbound, dizzy, waiting for the answer.

"Do you really want this?" she asks again, and holds up the altered photograph of the two of us, cheek to cheek: two little suns about to collide, one destined to steal the energy away from the other.

The photos fall. The blue vanishes. The ringing rhythm goes dead, and there's a hand on my shoulder. Steve. He cuts my call and even though I can feel him right behind me, his voice is inside my head, split seconds behind his just-behind-me voice.

"Sid-Sid. Don't-don't you want this-this?" He pats my shoulder. "You-you really got to want this, man-man." He flips up his mic and squats down next to me. "You okay? You're spacing out on me, brother."

"Sorry, Steve. I was waiting for The Randomizer to kick in."

"It's down."

"Right."

"That's why the numbers are up on your monitor."

"Gotcha."

"Where they've been for the past ten minutes."

"Sorry."

He stands up and chucks my shoulder again. Hard.

"Don't be sorry, Sid," he says, and clicks his omniscient control back on. The squawk of the feedback makes me jump. "Just dial the numbers."

My dog, Zero, and I are in the living room, staring out the picture window at our street-side mailbox. We're trying to determine if the mail has arrived yet. Normally we'd just walk out to look, but the neighbor kid across the street is in her yard, and she's a talker.

"What do you think?" I ask Zero.

He blinks a few times, feigning disinterest. He's definitely not jumping at the door.

"Me too," I tell him.

The neighbor kid's name is Mary Jo. She's maybe nine or ten. She stands at the edge of her yard, leaning hard against her mailbox. She does this a lot. The box appears to be growing out of her armpit, attached, cementing her to the ground.

"She's not leaving, you know that," I tell Zero.

He sighs, and reluctantly rises to all fours.

I open the door and we begin our walk, both of us trying to look focused, preoccupied with a specific mission, exuding great purpose. It doesn't work.

"Hey," she yells across the street. She stares at me through squinty eyes. It's overcast, but she still squints at me.

"Hi," I say, and keep walking.

She tilts her head back a notch and looks down at me, as if she's wearing bifocals. "You're a weird one," she says.

"How's that?"

"You, with the postcards."

I look in my mailbox to see two new arrivals. It's a little unsettling that they're coming in pairs now: Luxembourg and Austria this time. I think about Gerald the Post Office Guy's warning of tricksters and look back at Mary Jo, who is clearly not exhibiting great respect for her mailbox—she's practically hanging on it. But is this the posture of a serious criminal? Can someone her age be a mastermind?

"How old are you?"

"Ten."

"Do your parents know you abuse their mailbox?"

"Mailboxes are the property of the U.S. government," she says, "and I'm not abusing it. It's got a six-foot post that goes into the ground, and my grandfather put it there and he said even a tornado wouldn't move this mailbox."

"Where's your grandfather now?"

"Florida," she declares, as if I should be impressed. "I might go live with him someday, because there aren't any kids around here to play with, and I can't leave the yard while my parents are at work, but I do know every cat in the neighborhood. Do you have a cat?"

"Well," I start, and Zero grumbles, but she talks right over both of us.

"There are seven, and their names are Cinderella, Sparkles, Ginger, Sunshine, Sassafras, Unicorn, and Princess."

"A cat named Unicorn? Really? That sounds made up."

She squints at me again. "You're weird. You, with the post-cards."

"What do you know about the postcards?" I ask.

"You know," she says. "Yooou know," she sings out.

I think about this. "You're funny," I say, circling my finger at the side of my head the way kids do to indicate crazy.

"Me," she says, practically in italics, then jabs her finger hard into her breastbone. "Me?" she says again, her voice laced with cruel implication.

I decide to give Gerald the Post Office Guy another try at explaining my postcard mystery. I think he might have been rushed last time.

I find my place in line, content to watch other customers as they drop off packages or collect their stamps. It's eventually my turn, and no one is behind me. And while I don't have anything to deliver, the more questions I ask the more Gerald seems okay with chatting. He talks to hear the sound of his voice, and I listen for the same reason. His philosophical meanderings are entertaining and there is something comforting about knowing someone is in charge. I ask him about faraway regions, places where deliveries might be difficult or easily botched.

"Alaska's especially challenging," he says. "It's beautiful, but so remote."

I nod, fascinated.

"There are parts of Alaska where our guys use snowmobiles."

"No."

"Oh yeah. Ever since the Homeland Security Act, parcels that received payment for ground delivery need to stay on the ground. No Cessnas flying those packages. Our guys use snowmobiles."

Our guys. I like that. Like he's a part of a real team, something bigger, that gets big things done. Like the armed forces, without the arms or force.

"But overall, Air Priority is the best route no matter what you're sending," Gerald says. "It's a good way to go."

"I like the good way."

He smiles, and clears his workspace of paper scraps. Several new customers make their way in through the glass doors.

"Pretty unique ways to deliver," he says.

Have they considered moose, I wonder.

"Have a good day," he says.

I walk away to make room for the new customers. After a few steps, I really want to share the moose line with Gerald, so I turn back. But he's already asking a lady if she's sending anything liquid, perishable, or fragile.

At the time of my father's death, my family lived together under one roof. I was twelve and Natalie was sixteen. Mom was figuring out how to manage life with no husband and two kids, and it was tough because there were always reminders that he was gone. Not like photos or old clothes, but less obvious things that couldn't be boxed up or thrown away. They were welcome and crushing at the same time. For months we'd get phone calls from telemarketers asking to talk to Dad. And that wasn't cool at all because whoever answered the phone had to explain.

And there were the more subtle mementos, like the copper pipes. Dad was a plumber, and he had fitted our house with copper pipes, the best kind to use for plumbing. He taught us the virtues of copper piping: versatility, strength, durability in extreme temperatures, biostatic qualities that don't allow bacteria to grow. He talked to us like we were adults, coconspirators in his mission to convert every house in town to copper piping. "You get what you pay for," he used to tell me, and also "Copper is a little more expensive but worth it in the long run," and "There's no way we'll use anything but copper in our house."

I was a bit mystified by my dad's white work truck, how the interior was lined with long sections of shiny pipe, the copper color morphing from brown to orange to red in the sun. He was like an alchemist to me, shaping and shifting metals, casting spells on homes by infusing them with his special brand of invincibility.

I used to think that the water we drank was better than our neighbors' because we had copper pipes. It was a great secret I kept from my friends. And for a long time after Dad died, I thought about him every time I turned a faucet.

Other reminders of Dad were literally sent to our house. Junk mail arrived for him daily, which was unsettling at first because he wasn't there to tear it up and grumble about it. But we got used to it. It was weirdly comforting to know that Dad was important enough to have been solicited for cable television and lawn care and someone's vote for office. In a strange way, the junk mail had made us feel he wasn't far away, like there was a fleeting chance he might still be around. We actually missed it when it stopped coming.

But telemarketers were never welcome.

Sometimes I could tell when the phone was for Dad because Mom would mutter something into the receiver and then slam it down. "Who called?" we'd ask. "No one," my mother would say. Then she'd look at us and repeat it with great conviction. "It was no one." Just like in the movies, when one character asks another what they'll do now that something terrible has happened, like a plane's pilot dying of a heart attack mid-flight. "What do we do now?" a passenger inevitably asks. "Don't know," the character answers. Their gaze drifts into the distance and they repeat what they just said, as if repeating it brings a deeper, more serious meaning. "I just don't know."

I'm doing it again, the car-wash thing. It's raining hard outside and I'm inside my car, which is inside a small cinder-block building. I'm watching the spot-free rinse spill down my windshield, and several feet away the autumn rain is streaming down the windows of the car wash. I can't tell if I'm outside or inside. It doesn't matter. I bought ten car-wash codes and I'm doing laps. There's no line because of the weather, so it's all mine.

A simplicity exists within the touchless system that relaxes me, the way the robot arm works its way around my car in perfect quadrants, spitting pink foam and rinsing with such precision. There is a challenge to getting my car automatically dried in less than the sixty allotted seconds of high-velocity air spewing from the three black throats of the ceiling fans—I'm sure the entire front half of my car is dry when the rainfall spots the hood and it's time to drive back to the beginning.

Zero comes with me sometimes. He's so laid back about everything, but he can barely stop from wetting himself when we do the car wash. If he knew I did laps like this, he would never be able to contain himself. I left him home today.

I like it in here because nobody can reach me on my cell

phone and the four-and-a-half-minute cycle is short enough that there's nothing else to do but sit. I like it in here because my car is clean and there are no postcards. I like it in here because I know where I am and I know where I am going.

Outside, a clearing has cut through the clouds, and through it the sunset is visible. Two cars have already lined up at the car wash; my lone reign is officially over. Good thing the codes are good for thirty days. I finish my last drying cycle and drive down the road. I study the sunset in my peripheral vision.

I've been watching sunsets lately, to see what the big deal is. As a rule, I like them. I respect their beauty and punctuality, and I'll admit to an occasional feeling of awe when the colors are just so. What I mean about the big deal is that so much has been laid on the sunset—heavy-handed metaphors, sentimental music. Everyone's always walking into them, and that is some very intense light. Maybe that's where the term "love is blind" comes from, because so many people are walking into sunsets, burning out their corneas.

Often in the movies, the sunset image is shoved in my face so I'll be sure to know what to feel. I'll admit to enjoying a large number of Westerns that have ended this way. Maybe I've even welled up a little when the cowboy rides off with the girl—a perfect moment, a just life, a popcorn reminder of how things should be. See: "sunsets, riding into the—" My problem is, I'm watching a sunset right now, in all its washed-out oranges and reds and purples. It's like the sun is hiding behind a sky-sized blanket of pastel colors, burning bright enough to let me know it's there, but not enough to be postcard material. And this sunset is in my story, but I'm not sure what to make of it. No music is playing, no girl or horse is hanging around. And while it's pretty to look at, tonight it's what I would describe as lethargic.

There was a time after Mom died and before Natalie got married that I moved out of our childhood home to live with Zoe. The bedroom was described as cozy in the classifieds, which meant tiny. It was a room with a bed in it. Zoe and I liked it that way; we called it our nest.

We found most of our nest décor at The Big Bazaar antique shop, a two-level extravaganza of furniture, knickknacks, and oddities. The main floor was stocked with vintage clothing, old musical instruments, and heirloom dressers. Glass cases displayed various collectible magazines, political buttons, playing cards. The basement had retro-hip curiosities: pachinko machines, jukeboxes, shag rugs, and couch-sized phonograph systems.

During our first visit, Zoe was immediately drawn to an atrocious wood-framed painting that depicted a man rowing a gondola. She held her arms out game-show style to highlight its magnificence. "Perhaps this artifice we shall call 'The Gondolier' is in favor of your purchase?" she asked in an Italian accent.

"That's terrible."

"Isn't it? Most people in Venice use *vaporetti* anyway—water buses. Did you know the city actually stretches across more than one hundred small islands?"

"How do you know these things?" I asked, shaking my head.

She put her arms down but continued to study the painting as I hovered over the glass cases.

I remember thinking while we walked around downstairs: Here we are, shopping for our first home item together, and it just might be a rusty old tuba or a chair shaped like a hand. Fantastic.

We ended up buying a set of heavy red curtains with gold fringe on the bottom. I was happy because they reminded me of a movie theater. Zoe was happy because they made her feel like we were living someplace more exotic than we actually were.

In that cramped little bedroom, we filled the gaps between the mattress and the wall with pillows and layers of blankets. The massive curtains also served as a great way to block out the sun. All that padding made the place almost completely silent, like a well-lined tomb.

I remember once she and I were lying in bed together, her small body spooned in behind mine. My eyes were closed and I could hear her whispering as she lightly ran her fingers up and down my spine. The motion made my skin tighten and chill. I opened my eyes. I wondered if she heard the soft pull of my eyelashes, it was so quiet in there. I stared at the wall before me, and she kept up the hushed tones, the tracing of my skin.

"What are you doing?" I whispered to the wall.

She hummed a random melody, as if I'd never asked the question, and continued to draw odd shapes on my back and shoulders and arms. "I'm memorizing you," she finally said. She grabbed my right hand and studied it intensely, brushing her palm against it, gentle repetitions to match her little song. I felt so happy that she'd want to memorize me. I felt like God had given me a gift.

But I knew what she was doing. This was another piece of Zoe's cryptic puzzle that, when finally assembled, would reveal the reality that she and I would not always be together. It had never been explained why this was our destiny, but she said things like this to me on a regular basis, like she was waiting for my departure, that separation was a natural, inevitable stage in our relationship. The funny thing is, I think I finally understand she was right. People never stay together forever. If they don't break up or divorce, one will die first, leaving the other in pain. And Zoe knew.

"What would you do if I were dead?" she'd sometimes ask, usually while standing by the stove if I was cooking, or next to the sink if I was shaving.

"I'd be miserable."

She'd look around the room and rock on the balls of her feet, building up to what promised to be a hugely philosophical moment. "I'm cute," she'd say.

"Beautiful," I'd remind her.

Then she'd stare at me like she thought I was lying. "You'd miss me. A lot."

"I know," was my conclusion.

It was times like this, in bed with the memorization game, that Zoe made it clear the puzzle was quickly coming together. Either I was to make a grave mistake or something terrible was to happen to her. Those were our unspoken options. Maybe that's just how I see it now, given everything that's happened.

The postcard I receive next has a photo of a sunset. It's the kind of image travel magazines use on their covers to lure readers into discovering the location of the miracle light. I catch myself looking over this one a few seconds longer than I did the other postcards. Something about this image, the pure energy of the rays cutting through primeval clouds, the authoritative tone of all things majestic. It's Biblical. Prophetic.

The postcard came from New Jersey.

The back has a coupon for a free oil change from the Sunny Smiles Garage in Hoboken, and I feel like I've been there before. Maybe when we visited Manhattan? I figure I must've been put on a mailing list, but then I see my name's been written by Zoe's hand.

So I do the only thing I can do. First, I make sure Zero has food and water. Then, I get in my car and drive. I figure if I'm in the car driving, I can always argue myself out of going all the way to New Jersey. I'll have twelve hours to make my case. Even if I lose the debate, all that time won't be lost on the road.

After four hours of arguing with myself, I realize I'm two states away. I succumb to the rest of the drive. About eight hours into my journey, I feel guilty for having left Zero alone. He'll be okay; there's a two-way dog door to the backyard, and I'll be home soon. But something else is bothering me. It's the hum of the highway, the false feeling of security everyone has as they smoke cigarettes, eat cheeseburgers, drive with one finger. The way they don't pay attention to what's in their peripheral vision, and how they listen to talk radio and laugh at invisible voices as the divider lines slip by them one by one—dash, dash, dash.

When I finally find Sunny Smiles, I'm not smiling and it's not sunny. A thunderstorm has just passed through, leaving the pavement steamy. The air is muggy and thick, and the pregnant black clouds have been reduced to light gray clouds. Wet tires hiss past me as my car crawls up the street.

The building itself looks more like a mall or an amusement park than an automotive garage. The quick oil change is connected to a car wash that is connected to a Laundromat with an arcade inside and coin-operated circus animals to ride outside. Connected to that is a bar. I guess something for the whole family was the thinking behind this little oasis. The outer wall is painted with a mural of a smiling cartoon sun floating in a bright blue sky with happy clouds and twittering birds. It all seems out of place. I'm already disappointed.

The postcard's image is nowhere to be seen. Clearly the picture on the garage wall is not the same as the photograph, and from the looks of the weather, there won't be any miraculous sunscapes manifesting anywhere nearby. Which also makes me think that there will be no Zoe nearby. I have driven nine hundred miles to get an oil change.

I park, get out of my car, and walk over to the Laundromat. I insert a ten spot in the change machine, fill my pockets with quarters, and get a Cherry Coke from the vending machine. A miniature dolphin ride waits empty only a few feet away, and I figure why not, there's no harm in riding a little dolphin every once in a while. As I rock back and forth, I study the car wash adjacent to the garage. It's a stop-and-spray manual deal, just not the same as the old touchless, so no laps today.

A voice from above tells me I'm a clown. I look up. "Excuse me?"

"What are you, a clown? That ride's for kids. You're going to wreck it."

An irate mother has descended from the land of the laundry. She isn't amused by my occupation of her son's coveted dolphin. I stand up and offer the ride to the boy. They both study me cautiously, like I might be setting a trap.

The loud woman holds her arm in front of her son. I step back, armed with my diabolical Cherry Coke. I decide it's time to go talk to the mechanic.

Corey is the garage clerk, a small man with close-set eyes and messy black hair, and he offers to extend the expiration date on my oil-change coupon after I tell him my story and how far I've driven. He seems to feel genuinely bad that the coupon is a year overdue. That, and he's very concerned about being honest with me.

"To be honest with you," he keeps saying.

"So you don't remember ever seeing me here with a girl?" I ask.

"To be honest with you, I haven't been here that long. I wouldn't remember you or your girlfriend."

I wonder what he's being when he doesn't preface his sentences with this. I think about pulling out the photo of Zoe I've brought along, but decide to keep it in my pocket after his last answer.

"Couldn't you look me up on your computer?"

"They're down. We're doing all paper receipts today." Corey holds up a notebook with greasy fingerprints on it.

I try to engage Corey in shop talk to get away from my embarrassing situation. I ask him about starters and ignition systems.

"To be honest with you," he says, "Tom over there is the mechanic, I just run the register and manage phones. Honestly though, I've been learning a lot by watching."

Now Corey is embarrassed for being a garage clerk instead of a mechanic, while I stand there feeling like an idiot for driving to Hoboken over a postcard. Corey chews on his thumbnail while I feign interest in Tom's handiwork.

"Tell you what," I say, "if you or your mechanic remember anything or find anything on your computer, give me a call." I write my cell phone number on a Sunny Smiles business card and hand it to him.

He seems grateful, like he wants to give something back. "Hey, you like calendars?" he asks, and bends down behind the counter. He pops up with a Sunny Smiles Garage calendar emblazoned with the portentous light I saw on the postcard. "You can have one. Give you something to look at in the meantime. The oil change should only be about twenty minutes."

"Thanks." I walk outside and turn the calendar in my hands. On the back are twelve squares: a month for every smiling girl. They are all bikinis and bright eyes, brilliant white teeth and slippery skin, every photo full of glossy luminescence.

A hydraulic press exhales and groans behind me, a car rising on the lift. I turn to see if it's mine, but it looks like I'm next. I catch a whiff of oil and metal, and then some unexpected smells:

peanuts, chips, cigarettes. It's the bar attached to the Laundro-mat attached to the garage. I've got time to burn, so I continue my investigation.

The front door is mostly glass, with the name MICKEY's etched across it. A shamrock punctuates the design, but the interior doesn't resemble any Irish pubs I've seen. There are no fire-places, no massive wooden beams. It's merely a big square room full of tables and chairs, booths against the walls. The bar itself is pushed off to one side. An Irish flag hangs behind it, a weak at-tempt at homeland pride. The bartender is a tiny man, his shoul-ders barely clearing the bar's counter. He washes dishes with great intent, hardly noticing I've arrived. The three patrons on the other side of the room don't seem to notice either.

I walk up to the bar and fish out the photo of Zoe from my pocket. It's a Polaroid picture, the self-portrait of me and Zoe taken on one of those days we were bored and decided to screw around and make something zany. She knew how to scratch at the film as it developed, and she created some wild squiggly designs around our faces—strange glyphs that punctuated our mood of the day. Not the most normal image, but still the clearest photo I have of her face.

"What can I do you for?" the bartender asks.

I'm startled by his sudden appearance. My peripheral vision didn't catch his approach. I spin the photo toward him. "I was wondering if you remember seeing the girl in this photo?" I real-ize I'm acting like a TV cliché, showing photos to bartenders, but it seems to be working.

"You a cop?" he asks.

"No. Does it matter?"

He smiles and shrugs. "Not really. Just always wanted to say that." He picks up the photo and gazes at it, his expression full of forced contemplation. He nods slowly and scratches his chin. I get the feeling he's milking this episode for everything it's worth. Probably not much excitement going on at the Mickey's Laundro-Garage-Bar.

"So, does she look familiar?"

He bites his lip and raises his eyebrows. "Oh yeah, I remember this girl," he says, and brushes a thumb across the scratch designs.

I take the photo back. "You sure you've seen her here?"

"Looks like that one over there," he says, and nods across the room where a young, dark-haired woman sits. She's fair-skinned and thin, like Zoe. I can see how this guy might make the comparison. I put the photo back in my pocket and study the bartender's eyes. They are alive, glassy, like a woodland creature: tender, afraid. I wonder if he notices this when he looks in the mirror, if he's at all aware of his fragile nature.

"How long ago did you see her?" I ask.

"Maybe a year ago sometime, I can't remember."

"But not recently?"

"No."

"A year is a long time," I say. "How can you be sure?"

"I remember those freckles," he says, and taps his nose. "Very nice."

He's right. The nose freckles are one of a kind. Splashed across her face like a constellation of stars: five large, twelve small. I know the numbers because I used to count them. When I couldn't sleep, I would stare at her for hours while she was lost in slumber—mouth open, drooling on the pillow, like a child sleeps. I used to imagine a connect-the-dots game on her face, creating my own Zoe Star Systems. Crescent Major was the three large freckles on her left cheek, and the Tear Twins sat directly under her right eye in perfect alignment with the path her tears would follow. The other Minor Freckles I thought of as distant, mysterious suns never to be visited or understood by anyone—not even Zoe, not for several lifetimes. I used to wonder if even she understood what a marvel she was, lying so peaceful there in the dark, her eyes twitching with dreams.

"She dead?" he asks.

I hold my breath at this question, and wonder: is she? It's a good question, although not one I would ask a man searching for a missing person, especially if he was in the photo with her. "Missing," I say, and turn away so as not to catch his reaction.

Outside, the cloud bank has broken up. Giant fingers of light reach down to touch the earth. The rain has transformed the parking lot into a steaming slab of asphalt, a fog and light show. And although I'm on the edge of New Jersey, it feels like somewhere else.

Back home, Zero is not impressed with my travels. I tell him about Corey the garage clerk and his propensity for talking about honesty, but Zero gazes sadly out the window, his eyes glassed over on the verge of tears. Total drama. Pure melancholy.

"I did not abandon you," I say, and point at him for emphasis.

Zero glances over to the refrigerator calendar, then studies his empty bowl.

"That bowl was overflowing with food when I left. You gorged yourself to make me feel guilty."

His tail thumps defiantly.

I go to the answering machine, which blinks with a bright red number one. I push the button, and a robot lady voice tells me I have a message. It beeps and Natalie's voice comes out of the box: "Hi Sidney, I got word back from X-Ray. They said they could set up a CAT scan for you tomorrow. Give me a call and we'll make it happen. Remember, it's nothing to worry about."

Zero sighs heavily. First the abandonment, now this.

"It's not that kind of cat," I tell him.

I open the fridge and grab some leftover chicken, toss him a chunk as a peace offering. He warily sniffs at it, as if I've just thrown him poison. But ultimately he can't help himself and inhales the meat.

"It's really not what you think," I assure him, and wonder what the hell it is exactly, in my head, that's so messed up it needs to be scanned.

They keep telling me it's almost over.

I'm lying face-up on an ice-cold gurney, entombed inside a massive humming machine. An electric eye slowly spirals around my head, pausing for contemplation and an occasional blip or whir.

"It's almost over," they say again, muted voices from outside the tomb. "Don't move your head, just another minute."

The truth is, if I could buy tickets to this ride, I would. The only thing missing is the pink foam. I feel strangely calm here, with the electric eye blinking its meditative trance signal. I breathe in and out and the eye blinks in unison, and we come to an understanding, the eye and I. If it weren't so damn cold, I could lie here all day.

"Twenty seconds," someone says.

Good-bye electric eye, I think. It blinks back at me.

After the test, I sit in my green gown and wait for Dr. Singh's arrival. I study the black-framed diplomas on his wall: a bachelor's degree, a master's, an MD. Others describe specialties and boards, procedures and licensing. They're all ornately written in unreadable calligraphy, but they look impressive. One is perched unusually high on the wall but I can't read it. I'm about to stand on my chair to check it out, but Dr. Singh makes his entrance.

He sketches mad notes on my chart, short, dark hieroglyphs that are illegible maybe even to him. He doesn't look up. I sigh and drum my fingers on my knees. He mumbles some words to himself, flips a page back and forth, then looks up at me as if I'd asked him something. "You can get dressed. We'll have someone call you."

"Any chance you know when the results will be in?" I ask.

"We'll let you know when you get weak, probably right before you die," he says, and tucks his chart under his arm.

"Okay," I say, and hop off the ice-cold steel table onto the ice-cold tile floor. He leaves the room and I change back into my civilian attire. A giant calendar hangs on the door, decorated with illustrations of myriad microscopic diseases. I wonder how many of those four-inch-by-four-inch days it will be until I'm consumed by the little dots that clump together, or sunk into a coma by the long stringy things that interweave. The doctor walks by, and I wave him down. "Doctor?"

He stops and looks up from another patient's chart, this one full of jagged penmanship. "Yes?"

"Could you say that again?"

"About your results?"

"Yeah."

"As long as a week, probably closer to a day?"

"Thanks."

The doctor searches my eyes back and forth, back and forth, like the manic expressions of soap opera actors on Univision just before they shed tears. He talks softly then, but forcefully. "Let's not worry about anything until we see what we've got, okay? It might be nothing at all." His face changes then, possibly into what he feels is a compassionate smile, but it comes off as slight dental discomfort. He looks back at his chart and continues his purposeful walk down the hall.

I want to tell him that I'm sure it's really nothing too, and that I'm not worried about it. I want to assure him that the wild lilac bush in my head randomly blooms because of something unrelated to the medical field, and that whoever has a chart with extra dots on the *i*'s is probably in more dire need of his help. But I keep my mouth shut.

Outside the weather is gray and cold, much less pleasant than inside the giant humming machine. I walk to my car, and inside is the bag of postcards. I pick one at random. London Bridges, it says. It's as good as the rest of them, I think, and immediately know that a Wanderlust #15 will do the trick. I congratulate myself on selling one more vacation package. It's time to cash in on my flex-time privileges, and make use of that employee discount. I'll tell Steve I'm doing some guerrilla-style vacation research; he should be thrilled.

"You forgot all about me," a voice cries.

I sit up in bed. My alarm clock rests innocently on its night stand, quiet as can be, so the voice probably woke me again. It's dawn, or near it, as evidenced by the slats of orange light penetrating the window blinds. I shade my eyes. I've got to get some curtains.

"All of you forgot about me," the voice says. It's my mother, whimpering in an uncharacteristically desperate tone. A whine is more like it, but laden with true grief, real suffering. It's coming from the wine bottle under the stairs. A whine from the wine.

I get out of bed and make my way to the basement, down the carpeted stairs, following the voice. The lilacs that sometimes bloom in my head often accompany her voice, and I guess that makes sense, given how much she loved those flowers, although I'd never tell that to Dr. Singh or Natalie. And while the scent can be disconcerting, her voice is less of a threat, due to its predictability and sheer repetition.

"How could you all forget me?" she asks.

"Nobody forgot about you," I say. "We could never forget you."

Her voice changes to a finger-shaking tone. "I don't remember telling anyone that this was okay with me," she says, "but people do what they want."

I believe it's better not to respond, so I keep quiet and listen. I'm concerned about committing too much energy arguing with alcoholic beverages.

The bottle is a '67 Bordeaux, plainly labeled with blue print on white paper. My mother's spirit is trapped inside. I know this because I moved the bottle from the bottom rung of my wine rack to another location entirely—under the staircase and behind the box of green army blankets. The voice followed. I heard her muffled crying a second time and was hoping it might be something more acceptable, like a lost kitten or stray squirrel baby, but it was Mom, cooing and whining under the stairs, alone in the dark. I guess she stuck close to this particular bottle because she and my father had kept it as an anniversary gift, never really intending to open it.

I like to think her soul lives inside the bottle, like a genie who might get drunk on occasion, and this would explain her crying spells in the afterlife. She was never much of a complainer. But I wonder if all this afterlife drama is making up for her lackluster departure. She died so suddenly and silently, without warning or fanfare. No last words, no calling out to Jesus.

When I was in middle school, one of the kids in my class died by drowning. I always thought this was a dull way to go, silent and futile, probably with nobody nearby for rescue, hence the drowning part. It sounded so lonely and anticlimactic. So I made a list of exciting ways to die. It went like this:

1. Avalanche
2. Massive Explosion
3. Lightning Strike

4. Plane Crash
5. Gang Warfare / Hand-to-Hand Combat
6. Shark Attack
7. Roller-Coaster Malfunction
8. Industrial Turbine Accident
9. Spontaneous Combustion
10. Death by Fear

All of these involve lots of screaming and violence and terror, which seemed to be the best way to go at the time. But when Mom died, it was quick and quiet, like a lightbulb turned off. A flick of the switch. Personally, I would take the switch in a heartbeat now. But Mom was a mover. So maybe she's getting out all her guilty pleasures now, and she's going to cry and moan to me every morning at 6:15 a.m. until she gets it out of her cosmic system. I like the company, but it's hard to explain to others.

"She told me if we saw the sun set enough times," I tell Zero, "we would eventually forget about her and she would disappear forever."

Zero sits, staring up at me, seeming to accept and understand.

"She's really worried about this, and she won't be consoled," I say. "You want some coffee?"

Zero wags his tail. I pour us each a cup of black and sugar. He holds his nose over the coffee and drools through a smile. He's clearly not worried about my ghost story.

"You knew about her before I did, didn't you?" I ask.

Zero lifts his eyebrows, then flattens them out, a little embarrassed.

"So why didn't you tell me?"

He laps up his coffee and sits back on his haunches.

"Didn't want to worry me, eh?" I nod. "Good ol' Zero. Things are worse than they seem, though."

He's not impressed with my dramatic statement. He walks in circles a few times and lies down, wrapping his tail around himself. He looks up at me with sad eyes and his whole body moves as he sighs.

"I know worry doesn't help anyone, and I also know that I shouldn't be having conversations with you beyond asking you for a walk."

Zero's tail betrays him with a sudden thumping.

"Cut it out," I say. "I'm going to have to go away for a little while, do some research. So that means a short stay at Sunnyland Kennel for you."

Zero's tail stops; he promptly stands on all fours, his body stiff with this unfortunate and unexpected turn of events.

"Unless you want to go to Europe."

I spread the postcards out before him, picture-side down so he can see all the messages from Zoe. He gazes at them for a few moments, looks up at me, then circles himself again to lay down by the fire, and stares into the flames.

I read once that the reason dogs circle around before they lie down is to trample all the snakes in their grass bed so they can sleep in peace. Zero doesn't look particularly peaceful. I decide to have Natalie take care of him while I'm gone and spare him the tortures of the Sunnyland Kennel.

I cup my hand over the phone and hope Nat can't hear the wailing. But it's too late, she's already asking me what all the noise is about. It's more difficult than you think to disguise the distinct rise-and-fall cry of an English police car.

"Just watching the telly," I say.

"The *telly*?" she asks with a hard edge of sarcasm.

Nothing gets by Natalie. It's amazing how quickly I've assimilated into London culture, all the way down to their manner of speaking. I wonder if my own sister even knows it's me. It's possible she thinks this is an elaborate prank brought on by someone other than myself—a villain or criminal, a mastermind postal offender.

"Sid?" she asks. "What's going on?"

"Oh I'm just calling to tell you I'm feeling much better. I mean, the smells stopped and all."

"That's good news."

"Yeah." I clap my hand over the phone again. The police car must be going through a roundabout because it's headed back my way, bawling like a baby toward the hotel. Eeeh Aaah Eeeh Aaah. Natalie notices the gap in our conversation.

"Are you sure you're okay?"

"Oh, right. Yes. Brilliant."

"Uh-huh. And why are you using a phone card?"

"Sorry?"

"The phone card number. It came up on my caller ID."

I think about this. I can't tell her I'm in the London Hyatt that processed Zoe's first postcards because she will either not believe me or, worse, she will believe me, and as I've said before, she would have me committed in a heartbeat. It's best to keep things simple.

"Oh, the phone card thing," I say breezily. "I just thought it might be cheaper to use one instead of paying all those long-distance bills."

"You live two miles away."

"Right." So much for simplicity. "I'm actually in the UK on a secret mission to uncover a mail-fraud criminal, and I thought a phone card would be cheaper."

"Good one. I'm glad to hear you're feeling better," she says. "What's up?"

"Can you take care of Zero for a couple of days? I'm visiting some friends, and don't want him to panic."

"Of course. Why didn't you just bring him over? Zero loves it here."

The truth is, Zero can't stand it at Natalie's house. Her husband, Jake, spends most of his time on the Internet and they have a Siamese cat that sits on the most comfortable furniture and stares at Zero with savage contempt for hours on end. Zero was shocked to be victim to such drawn-out hostilities. He thought cats slept sixteen hours a day. Not this one.

"If you could just stop by and make sure he has food and water, that'd be great. The key is inside the fake rock."

We wrap up our conversation and I stare out the tall windows of my hotel. The city of London allows itself to be gazed upon like a beautiful woman posing naked for a portrait: full of mystery, hungry for adulation, waiting for something magical to happen.

First, it's the yelling. The man behind the double-thick glass walls shouts something at me, but I swear it's not English. I am in London though, and what else would they be speaking here? I'm at a currency exchange booth, so isn't he required to speak several languages? He yells again and then he starts the pointing. Yelling and pointing. He never looks at me, only down at the sliding glass tray. Next he talks loud and slow, like I'm a dumb foreigner, and I realize he is speaking English, but with a strong accent. The people behind me in line don't verbally complain, but a few shuffle their feet and cough. The man opens the sliding tray again, takes my money, and exchanges it for bills and heavy coins, then waves me out of the way. I'm not sure what just happened, but I'm glad I have money. I'm also glad that Zoe didn't send any postcards from Tokyo or Dubai or Rio because I would really be screwed in a place like that.

After the money confusion, I decide to skip the tube system for now. I head out on foot, cruise the streets, keep my eyes open for Big Ben, Parliament, a post office. I feel suddenly more alive than ever before because I am completely out of place. Everything is new: the cobble of the sidewalks, the reversed flow of traffic, the big red double-decker buses. The coins in my pocket are heavy; they don't jingle as much as knock together. I'm fascinated by their weight, and I wonder why we Americans have such light money.

Down one street, I see several restaurants and a grocery. A man sits on a blanket in front of the grocery, a cup open and empty before him, waiting for donations. I walk over and drop my heavy coins—three of them—into the cup. They make an amazing thunking noise. He smiles up at me, then taps a sign he's made out of cardboard and marker. BE GRATEFUL, it says. I drop two more into the cup. What a great sound.

It's good advice: be grateful. I try to review my list of blessings as often as I can. My parents taught me to do that. Today I'm grateful I have a home, and food, and enough coins in my pocket to give away. Sometimes the list works. Sometimes it doesn't.

Sometimes I feel this ache inside over Zoe, and it won't go away. I imagine her sitting down to write these postcards and taking the time to stamp them and carry them off to a post office somewhere in a foreign land. I like to think of her in a cheesy souvenir shop, spinning the postcard towers around in circles, picking out the perfect one just for me—the one she knows will make me smile, the one that will make me think of her.

I create a new gratitude list:

I'm thankful I have lungs.

I'm thankful I can see.

I'm thankful for my dog.

And I am thankful for the postcards, but I still can't understand why Zoe left, why she won't call, why I can't find her, and how to make this ache go away.

The ache sometimes sits inside my rib cage. It feels like I took a cheap shot in a fight. Some days it will creep north and lodge itself in my throat, where it burns and swells. That's when I'm especially vulnerable, when even if I'm thinking happy thoughts or feeling hopeful, the burning lump makes itself known, a tangible reminder of something missing. A missing part. A missing person. Today I'm grateful the ache is sitting low under my ribs.

I gather up my courage and try out the tube subway system. It's not as complicated as I thought it would be, and with all the posted maps, I don't have to worry about anyone yelling and pointing at me. A recorded omnipresent voice reminds me to "mind the gap," which I am trying very hard to do. A busker plays a Beatles song, and while everyone else on the train seems annoyed, I find it comforting.

I visit the places I think Zoe might have gone. Piccadilly Circus isn't unlike Times Square with all its flashing lights and noise. There is a Chinatown here too, but it's not the same, it's smaller, it's all wrong. I spend some time in St James's Park, and buy a hot dog from a vendor. Zoe wouldn't let me buy any when we went to Central Park. She would hate that I'm eating meat from a cart.

Inside the phone booth it smells like soup. I'm afraid that the stench is emanating from the receiver, that the last person to use the phone was sick or a messy eater. I do my best to hover the phone a few inches from my face. This makes hearing more difficult on an already faded connection.

"Are you in a tunnel?" Natalie asks. Her voice, oddly enough, sounds like she could be in a tunnel. I picture her talking from one and wonder why she would think I was doing the same.

"Yes, I'm in a tunnel," I say sarcastically.

"It sounds like you're in a tunnel," she says, insistent.

"How's Zero?"

"He's fine. I think he misses you."

"Really?"

"He whines a lot."

"Sorry."

"He stares at me sometimes like he's waiting for something."

"He likes it when you talk to him."

"Do you ever give him treats?"

"Sometimes. I give him people food sometimes."

"That's terrible for dogs, you know. It's bad for their hearts."

"I know."

"Have you taken him to the vet for his annual? You should make sure he's got all his shots."

"Yeah, I gotta do that."

Natalie is silent for a moment, as if she's working something out in her head. "When did you get this dog again? I don't remember when you got the dog." The way she asks me, it sounds like she already knows the answer, like she's not concerned about the shots but something else.

"I don't know."

"No?"

I think about it for a moment. "He's been with me for a while, I don't know the exact date."

"Well that's okay if you can't remember."

"Did you hear back from the CAT-scan people yet?" I ask.

"They'll call you soon. Are you still feeling funny?"

"No change, really."

"Hm."

"What's that?"

"Nothing."

"No, that noise you made. Hm. You said *hm*. Why'd you say that?"

"It was a nothing noise. It meant nothing."

"Are you sure?"

"I'm sure," she says.

"Okay."

"Are you sure you're not in a tunnel?"

"No tunnel. Listen, I'll be home soon. I'll call you later. Say hi to Zero for me."

I quickly hang up before she can say anything because I don't like the six-stage good-byes: talk to you soon, have a good night, take it easy, good night, bye, good-bye. A Buddhist friend of mine from college never said good-bye to anyone because he believed that saying it meant saying good-bye to their spirit. He was always ending phone conversations abruptly or leaving unexpectedly. You only say good-bye when someone dies, he told me, so their spirit can leave and be at peace.

My feet are tired and my body achy from all
the walking in this cooler, damp weather.
The hotel's front lobby isn't much warmer,
and neither is the woman behind the front desk,
although she is terribly apologetic.

"Sorry?" she says, or asks, I'm not sure which. She's a short
little pear of a thing, with three perfect wrinkle lines running
parallel across her forehead. "Sorry?" she says again, tilting her
head at strange angles toward me. I realize I'm not speaking loud
enough, and that's her way of asking me to increase my volume.

"If I wanted to send a postcard to someone," I ask, louder,
"how would I do that?"

"You can leave it right here with us at the front desk," she
says, and smiles. The three lines smooth away, revealing a broad,
velvety forehead. Her skin is like some exotic fruit, ready to be
eaten. I think I'm hungry from all my exercise.

"Leave it right here?" I ask.

"Yes, that's correct, sir. We take the post out twice daily."

Tucked away on the back counter is a basket filled with letters. They look like they've been there awhile. "So where does it
go from here?"

"Sorry?"

"Where," I say even louder, "does it go from here?"

"I can hear you, sir, I just don't understand your question."

"I mean, does it go to a post office?"

Her smile remains constant, her voice pleasant and professional. I really like her demeanor. She reminds me of Gerald, the postmaster back home.

"Right, sir, it goes through the Royal Mail."

The Royal Mail. That sounds serious. Trustworthy. A place to get answers. "And where would I find a Royal Mail office?"

The three little lines on her forehead return, darker than before. "Did you have a problem or concern?" she asks. "Did we mishandle a parcel of yours?"

"Not exactly. I'd just like to visit this Royal Mail."

"Right, sir. Well, there are over forty-five offices in London. Which would you prefer?"

When she mentions the large number of locations, a tingling pain surges up my feet. I imagine bumbling along more cold, uneven sidewalks and realize I don't have the energy for any more travels today. "I'll get back to you on that," I say, and take the elevator up to my room, where I draw a hot bath and submerge myself. Pure healing. I soak with my ears below the water line, feeling no gravity and hearing nothing but my grateful lungs moving in and out underwater. I think about how I got here, in this English bathtub, alone in a hotel room on another continent.

Relaxed. Floating. I do something I do a lot. I replay the events of the day that first French postcard came.

It was a sunny afternoon, six months ago. A warm breeze was blowing, and I was innocently retrieving the mail.

"What you got there?" squeaked a voice from across the street. It was Mary Jo, Mailbox Monitor. She had her hands on top of her mailbox and her feet at the bottom post, curving her back to form a giant letter D.

"Excuse me?" I asked.

Mary Jo squinted back. "What'd you get in the mail?"

I looked at the pastoral view on the postcard: a field of daisies. *Bonjour!* it read. *Have a Nice Day.* Ridiculous. "Nothing."

Mary Jo sat down and lay back on her lawn, her feet still touching the mailbox, a giant letter L. "L is for lawn. I'm on the lawn!" She laughed hard at this, couldn't stop laughing. She was really laughing away.

I walked back toward the house, detouring to the trash can in my driveway. "L is for lost," I said, lifting the lid off the trash can and tossing the postcard in the garbage. Later, when Mary Jo had gone inside, I went back out and retrieved it.

The French postcards: Nice, Lyon, Paris. They had come right in a row. She was on a regular Tour de France. My "I See London I See France" vacation package from work (#15) only allows a trip to London and Paris. So, technically, it should be called "I See London I See Paris," but I guess that isn't as catchy. I could look into visiting the other cities in France, but right now the altered state of sensory deprivation in my hotel bathtub is something I don't want to interrupt. I soak for another hour, and then cocoon myself in the bed under heavy hotel blankets. I'm lost under their weight, my body falling fast asleep in a heady fog of linen and cheap soap.

The next day I wake up late. After noon, to be precise, and that means I'm not making it to the Royal Mail because I need to get to Heathrow to catch my flight to Paris. And that's okay because France is really where I think things will come together.

I'm not loud and I'm not rude, so I don't necessarily stand out as the quintessential Obnoxious American Tourist, but this French postmaster is clearly messing with me.

"Ah-lo!" he yells, then waves at me. "Ah-lo?"

He looks an awful lot like Gerald. His uniform is a darker blue than its American counterpart, as if he might take himself more seriously than Gerald, if that's possible. But he's got the same slate skin-tone and those spooky gray eyes. I wonder if postmasters are part of something larger, like some Jungian archetype of Messenger—a man created by the collective thoughts of humanity to deliver all written communication between all the souls of eternity.

He snaps his fingers in the air, like I'm a dog.

I stare into his creepy eyes. "I'm here," I say.

He squints after registering my American accent, then points at my hands. *"Qu'est-ce que c'est?"*

What's funny is that I heard him have a perfectly coherent conversation in English as I was waiting in line, and now that I'm directly in front of him, he's forgotten the language altogether. I decide to humor him.

"Sorry, I don't speak French," I offer. "Do you speak English?"

He nods, and says, "Mm." He studies me for a few moments, considering my clothes, my haircut, my willingness to wait for his answer. "What eez zeese?" he finally asks, and glances down at my hands again.

"It's a postcard collection," I say.

He pushes out his lips. *"Je ne comprends pas."*

"Post. Card," I say to him, loud and slow. I spread them out on the counter. I point at a postmark dated a year ago. Now I'm the yeller-pointer. "Can you explain this to me? The date?"

He picks up the card. "Zeese eez from one year ago," slipping into almost perfect English at the end. He shrugs, put off by the lack of challenge in my query. Nothing like Gerald. "Zeese eez all you need?"

"Why did it take a year for me to receive these?"

He studies me for a moment, looks behind me, and seems disappointed that nobody is waiting. He nods, backs up a step, and reaches for something under his counter. He pulls out a world map and unfolds it on the counter before me. *"Voilà,"* he says, and taps it to show me this is the answer to my question. "You zee? You zee zeese?"

"Yes," I say.

"What eez zeese?"

"It's the world."

"Oui. Le monde!"

"Le monde," I say, trying out my best accent. I've heard that if you at least attempt to speak the language, foreigners appreciate your humility, regardless of your fluidity. It works. He leans in closer.

"Your postcard, eet travels *le monde*, no?"

"*Sí*, it travels *le monde*," I say.

"*Oui*," he corrects.

"Wee," I say.

He frowns. "But you with zee postcards, you are not so happy zeese cards are from anozzer time, no?"

I'm starting to think that while the French postmaster may be a little unconventional in his tactics, he may have some useful information. I forgive his flamboyant performance and listen intently.

"You with zee postcards from anozzer time are wondering why zay arrive late to your home, *oui*?"

"Wee," I say. "Yes indeed."

"Mm." He raises an eyebrow, purses his lips over this predicament. It's obvious that he wants to share something, but for some reason feels it necessary to act out this little drama. "Yez, yez, yez," he says, then taps the map again. "Many cities have zee same name in all zee world. You know where eez Rome?"

"Italy."

"*Oui!* Eet *eez* een *l'Italie*," he says and smiles.

He points at the map again, this time at the Midwestern United States. "You know where eez zeese?" he asks.

"Wisconsin."

"Rome," he says, and quickly points to northern Europe.

"Finland?"

"Rome," he says, then lands on Italy.

"Rome?" I guess.

He points at me. "Yez. You zee?" He points to the sky to celebrate my revelation. "Rome eez een all different places een zee world—all of zem are Rome, but none of zem are zee same. But still, zee same name. Ah?"

"I don't get it," I say.

"You with zee postcards from anozzer time who does not get eet. Psh."

I study the map again to see if I can make better sense of it all.

"Eet eez zee problem avec zee *postal codes*," he says deeply. "Eef you write only zee city on a card as zee address, eet maybe goes to Canada even zough you want *l'Italie* or zee America. So zeese postcard, eet travels around zee world looking for you, and finally eet finds you, but eet eez much later zan zee expected time." He glances down at the *Have a Nice Day* card and notices something peculiar. "Zee? Zees one also goes to *Barcelone*. Eet travels zee world, zees postcard of yours. Eet eez stamped twice."

"I thought skip was illegal," I tell him.

"Who eez Skeep?"

I push the postcard toward him. "Are you telling me this one came from Barcelona?"

"*Oui.* Maybe eet was sent *par Paris*? Or maybe eet was purchased here, and sent from *Barcelone*?" He leans in closer. "Zee postcards do not care how zay arrive," he whispers. "Zay are only tiny pieces of *papier*."

I take back my card. This Barcelona possibility is the most infinitesimal clue imaginable, but I am filled with hope. "Thank you," I say. "I understand it much better now."

"*Vous ne comprenez rien,*" he says accusingly.

And as I gather up the postcards and shuffle them together, I can't help but think: Maybe I don't understand a thing.

In my hotel room, I turn on the television and I can't believe what's on. It's John the TV psychic, but he's overdubbed in French. What makes it even stranger is that there are English subtitles. John describes the process of translating his messages from those who've passed over. He actually says that it's like trying to translate English to French—sometimes there are words that don't mean the same thing, and you need to find a different way to express the message. Sometimes you can't get across exactly what needs to be said. Ever.

I wonder what I'm missing out on with the overdubs, what the network is leaving out in this translation. I wonder how much I'm missing out in general.

I decide I'd better check in with Natalie. She needs to know I'll be home later than planned, but she does not need to know it's because I ordered the "See Sexy Spain" overnight vacation add-on from Wanderlust. I'm not really one for club-hopping and discos, but it was the cheapest way to get to Barcelona. The pattern of her number on the touch pad makes the shape of half a house. She picks up. Zero barks in the background. He sounds anxious.

"How is everything?" I ask.

"Fine. Everything's fine."

"Is that Zero barking?"

A muffled sound and then clear air again. "Oh, he's just playing with Simon."

"Playing?" Last I remember, cats and dogs don't play together. Terrorize maybe. "So you're keeping him at your house?" That wasn't part of the deal, I want to say, but realize we didn't exactly write up a contract.

"Just for a little while. I'll take him back home tonight. What's up?"

"Just checking in."

"How are your friends doing? Catching anything?"

It takes me a moment to register what she means. Then I remember I told her some guys from work were having a fishing outing at their lake cabin. I don't remember which lake I said, though.

"No, we haven't hit the water yet. Just having a little party tonight."

"Are you at a party? It sounds awfully quiet."

"I just snuck inside to call. They're partying by the bonfire. Crazy animals."

"Oh," she says. "What's that?"

My hotel window is open and damn if there isn't an accordion on the street. I shut the window. "That's party music."

"Polka party? That sounded like an accordion."

"So I think I might stay another night if that's okay. We want to get out on the lake, since that's why we came. If that's okay."

"Oh," she says, then waits a little while before resigning. "Yeah."

"Great. Thanks, Nat. I owe you one."

"You owe me twenty," she says.

"Gotcha. Twenty," I say. The swooning accordion sounds pick up outside, so I try to end the call quickly. "All right then, good night."

"Good-bye. Talk to you soon," she says, and tries to sneak in a third and fourth farewell, but I hang up before she gets there.

The reason I'm so sure Natalie would have me committed is because she's done it before. She talked our mother into a short-term psych visit once. I'm not sure if it harmed or helped, but Natalie was behind the whole thing, whatever happened. At least that's how I remember it.

"I'm going into exile," Mom told me the night before she left, after having spent a couple of long hours talking with Natalie behind closed doors. Mom told me she "came to her own decision," but since then I've always been suspicious of my sister. Like now, she's waiting for me to crack, ready to sign the papers to put me into exile too, someplace where she'd know I was safe and she wouldn't have to worry about me while she takes care of her growing spawn.

Barcelona is brighter than I imagined. So much sun, it's almost overwhelming. The light is everywhere: it showers down from an impossibly blue sky, reflects off every building, glistens off every body. It slices up through the cracks in the sidewalks, fills up every corner, erases every shadow.

I heard about a disease people get from vacationing in places so beautiful they are psychologically incapable of handling it. Their intimate contact with pure unadulterated beauty makes them come apart at the seams. This may be such a place. I understand now why Zoe wrote "wish you were here." It's a bit unsettling, being alone in this sunny paradise. Maybe I'm just getting tired from all my travels—jet lag, and all that.

It takes me a while to get through the tight streets. There is so much brick and there are so many churches. I don't want to ask anyone if they speak English because I feel ridiculous asking *"Habla inglés?"* like I'm back in eighth-grade Spanish class and this is the magic phrase dumb Americans say because they're too good to learn a second language.

When I arrive at the Oficia del Postal, I am awestruck. This can't be the post office. A massive cathedral-like structure towers above me, with skyward spires and textures of an impossible pattern. It hurts to look at, it's so beautiful. I realize I've forgotten my sunglasses. I don't have a hat and I can't squint any harder. People pass me by and nobody speaks English. It's all gibberish. This whole place is noise and light and beauty. I decide to try the post office another time, when I'm better rested.

In the hotel gift shop, I look for some ibuprofen. There are shirts and hats and sunglasses and gum. There are shot glasses and candy and magazines. There is no ibuprofen. But there are postcards. Dozens of them, lining the shelves. I search through them and find an exact match to my Barcelona card. Adjacent to the postcards is a block of wood with a red pen attached to it by a string. The wood has writing all over it, scribbling from countless customers who used it as an ink tester. Zoe could have purchased her postcard right here and used this exact pen. I feel a surge of adrenaline with this thought, anxious about the close proximity of her presence.

I take the stairs back up to my room, jumping two at a time, and I think the effort forces too much blood to my head. My sunshine headache is evolving to something more substantial. I rarely get headaches, and this one is killing me. I want to call Natalie and tell her to take care of Zero in case I don't come back as planned. No way am I getting on a plane feeling like this. Maybe I'm being a little dramatic. Maybe I want to call Natalie just to hear somebody speak English.

I turn on the television for some distraction. I flip through the channels and John the TV psychic is not on any of them, thank God. The soap operas are plentiful, though, and they're all doing that manic back-and-forth face-searching. I wonder where they learned this style of acting. I turn the TV off, lie back in bed, and rub at my forehead. I think of Dr. Singh, how I still haven't heard back from him on the CAT-scan results, and how strange that day was.

"You know," the CAT-scan operator started to say that day, then let his words float unfinished in the room. I stood there in my little green gown, waiting for him to complete his out-loud thoughts. He was a tall, wiry guy with veiny forearms, probably younger than me, but he spoke as if he were the chief of surgery. MIKE, his name tag said in black plastic letters. "Paul McCartney helped pay for these machines to be made into mobile truck units," Mike said. "You're getting scanned with a little help from the Beatles." He grinned at his pun.

"I bet they're a bitch down the long and winding roads," I quipped.

Mike's face went blank.

I felt bad that he was trying to put me at ease. It meant he had compassion, and I was a big liar going to get scanned. It wasn't really a lie; I just wasn't meeting with the right person, maybe. I was wondering if an exorcist might be the more appropriate choice, but Paul McCartney probably didn't fund any mobile exorcism units.

"Hey," I offered, "did you know if you play one of the Beatles songs backward, it says 'Paul is dead'?"

MIKE strapped me onto the ice-cold gurney. "I'm not really a fan, actually," he said, slid up the safety rails, and rolled me into the belly of the giant humming machine. "It'll be over soon."

The curtains on my hotel room windows are maroon and delightfully thick, like the ones in movie theaters. I pull them closed and shut off all the lights. I push the bed up against one wall and surround myself with blankets and pillows. It's not the same as the nest I used to share with Zoe, but it serves its purpose as I wait for my headache to melt away.

I sleep for what must be several hours. When I wake, the daytime no longer creeps in around the edges of the curtains, which tangibly decreases the pain in my head. But my headache is replaced by a numbing boredom. With only four television channels to surf, I quickly cycle through my choices and realize it's time to get outside.

I open my "See Sexy Spain" vacation guide and study the photos: beaches populated with alluring models—uninterested women with dark tans, confident in their tinted eyewear; deeply tanned men with wraparound sunglasses, feigning indifference. Everyone is so cool, so apathetic. I need something to wake me up. I flip through more pages and find the *discotheque* section. I can't read most of the writing, but there are a lot of exclamation points and that looks exciting. According to one ad, a popular club is right up the street: Club de Cuerpo. I imagine Zoe might be drawn to such a place—an entire building filled with new, alluring people. Her interest in other cultures always showed itself for several days after we'd watch a foreign film. She'd talk about *discotheques* and *boulangeries*, stressing the correct foreign pronunciation to make those words stand out like works of audible art—as if their unique sounds were reason enough to visit faraway lands. I guess I need to see what all the noise is about.

My vision and hearing are officially gone. All I can sense is the thumping. A giant mass of soap bubbles has washed over me and most of the dance floor, like a horror-movie fog. The pulse is maddening, a physical presence infusing my internal organs. My hair vibrates. My eyes burn. Wild women whoop and swing their hair around and grind on other women.

It's a wild scene, but already I feel sick. Sick of this club, with all its strobe flashes and percussion bombs; sick of bright lights and brighter drinks—orange and lime-green concoctions created to poison the patrons; sick of the day and the night, the smell of suntan oil, the loud cooing of women trying so hard to appear like women who are having so much fun. Sick of myself and this hopeless journey.

My mouth waters, so I lean forward. I think: nobody will notice if I vomit. The soap machines will wash it all away. This disco is like a human carwash, but it is hot and miserable, not soothing at all. Two fun-filled coconut-oil girls make a Sid sandwich, polishing me with their bronze, bikini-clad buttocks. It all might be very exciting if the motion would cease and my eyes would stop burning and the pounding bass would quit shaking my stomach. I manage to slip through the crowd and squirm safely to a drier part of the club. I climb up two flights of stairs and perch on a dark balcony, high above the light systems and bubble machines.

From this view, Club de Cuerpo lives up to its name—not due to its beautiful bodies but because the club itself functions like a body. The entrance is the mouth, the dance floor the heart, the bars the stomach, the soap suds the liver, and the back alleyway the anus. The patrons are mere cells who move to the break-beat rhythm of DJ Brain, although not much of one considering the monophonic pulsing. So this must put me in the appendix, the organ which seems to have no purpose. Much better. Of course, the appendix is also known for rupturing suddenly and causing extreme pain and death, but at least my shirt's not vibrating.

I scan the crowd for faces, but I don't see Zoe or anyone even closely resembling her. I wonder if that's why she was initially attracted to this city. I wonder if she had as much fun as I'm having, or if she traveled to this exotic locale just so she could send a postcard.

Two twenty-minute super-song mixes later, it's time for me to leave. I descend to the main floor, where I see a security guy. At least someone's in charge. But this guy's not directing traffic; he's chatting up a model.

A drunk man by the front door shouts at a hulking bouncer. A fight breaks out. Hands push. Fists fly. A barstool catches air and an elbow jabs a fire alarm. The sprinkler system showers down cold, stale rain, and all *cuerpos* instinctively race for the closest exit. An entire body's contents flush out, regurgitated back onto the flashy streets of Spain, and me with them.

I am soaked, but no longer soapy. I walk across the street to separate myself from the crowd and observe the rest of the wet clubbers as they line the sidewalk. The women pull their long black hair back to squeeze out the water. The men peel off their shirts and tuck their them in the backs of their pants. People scream and laugh. The party never stops.

One of the girls breaks away from the pack and walks straight toward me. She's peculiar with her short blond hair. She has a cigarette in one hand, held awkwardly above her head to stop the water from streaming down her arm. Her other hand pulls her tight skirt down across tight thighs. Her heels click loudly on the street as she approaches. It's like watching a movie, until she speaks directly to me. Her words sound like Spanish or Portuguese. She rolls her eyes, looks back at her girlfriends, then says something again, this time in a different language, something harsher. Now she sounds Swedish, or maybe she only looks Swedish. I glance at her girlfriends. They wave. One of them blows me a kiss.

"Sorry," I say to the girl, "I don't understand. Do you speak English?"

"Do you have a letter?" the girl asks.

I raise my eyebrows. What does she know about a letter?

She laughs, puckers her lips, wrinkles her nose at me. "A letter? Do you have a letter?" She holds up her other hand and makes a gesture like she wants to thumb-wrestle me. Bizarre.

"Sorry," she says. "My English is no good. I am from Norvay. Do you know Norvegian?" She laughs as if she can guess the answer. Her friends blow me more kisses between their index and middle fingers. The Norwegian girl holds up her cigarette in front of her face. "I need a letter," she says, and loses her balance a little but catches herself. "Fire," she says.

"Oh," I say loud and slow, "a lighter!"

She points at me. Her friends cheer.

"Sorry, I don't smoke." I give her my best eighth-grade Spanish. *"No fumar. Lo siento."* I hold my palms up, and shrug.

She frowns in mock despair, then leans in toward me. "You are cute guy," she says, and kisses my cheek. She reaches out to touch my chin, gives it a gentle push, and says, *"Eso es desafortunado porque pienso te amo."*

"I don't speak Norwegian," I say, which is unfortunate.

She winks, spins around toward her friends, and clicks away.

Rotating the channels on my hotel television allows me to watch the pictures without watching them. I can stare bleary-eyed through the box of light while still gleaning some content. It's a nice break from the booming noise of the club, but my unfocused eyes are catching some weird stuff.

A commercial for Wild Chase Videos plays helicopter footage of cars smashing on the highway and flying off bridges. A World News channel displays an animation of space junk cluttering the stratosphere, crashing into satellites, hurling burned chunks of metal back toward the earth. The channels seem to have increased in number. A dog show has a woman sprinting alongside her purebred, the animal looking less than thrilled to be there. I swear the dog is somehow pleading for help, and when I snap my eyes back into focus, another commercial takes over the screen, advertising a deep-tanning lotion that makes you extra sexy.

I push the off button. The picture instantly reduces to a small bright square and hovers there for a moment, like it doesn't want to leave. I realize I've been at the edge of my seat for the past hour, my body rigid with engagement, regardless of my mental detachment. I roll my shoulders to loosen up. The little box of light dims.

I stand up to stretch, walk around the room a few times. I hear dogs barking at one another outside, or maybe they're barking at the moon.

I've noticed there are a large number of dogs running free in Spain, roaming the neighborhoods, weaving in and out of traffic. My late-night mind starts in with late-night thoughts: I wonder who picks up the animal carcasses left on the streets, if it's a job the police do in the earliest hours of the morning to avoid on-lookers. I wonder then who might pick up human carcasses, and how those people go home at night and manage to forget what they've seen when they tuck their children into bed, or make love to their wives before sleeping soundly. And do they sleep soundly? Or do they stay awake all night with the television on mute, half-watching blurry images of cars and satellites and dog shows, ruminating about morbid curiosities?

"All right, tiger," I say out loud, cutting off the stream of ominous thoughts, "time for night-night. Somebody's wiped out from too much excitement."

I go to the bathroom and run the shower, get back in bed, and listen to the white noise. My tired body falls unconscious almost immediately. I dream of car washes, giant humming tombs, pink foam sluicing down my windshield, gentle electric eyes blinking hello, and me, surfing on a strong, steady wave in the ocean of Deep Blue Bliss. Zoe memorizes my back with her fingertips and asks me what I would do if she were dead. I roll over to tell her what I always tell her, but her skin has turned to slate, she's cold to the touch. Her gray eyes stare lifelessly back at me. "Ning maa," she coos, and smiles.

Screaming in the middle of the night can draw attention. I don't know how long I've been doing it, but now that I'm awake, I feel hoarse, like I might have been yelling for the past ten minutes. I roll gingerly off the bed and tiptoe to the balcony. I peek over the edge. Nobody's looking up at me. I listen to the soundtrack of the room. It's quiet. No fists pounding my door. No cautionary phone calls. But then again, I'm in a foreign land. Maybe it's customary to let out an occasional nightmare-induced shriek, or, more realistically, to avoid the source of such a sound. Maybe I wasn't screaming at all. I could have been whimpering like a little girl, for all I know.

I venture a full look over the balcony, gaze down at the streets of Barcelona. An eerie, predawn quiet blankets the city. Only a scattering of cars peruse the normally chaotic roads. A few people stumble home from bars. A lone dog roams the sidewalk, sniffs, and pees randomly, as if marking the entire city as his own. I feel a strange urge to go downstairs and follow him. I wonder where he's been, and where he's going, or if he's just wandering aimlessly.

Suddenly I can't wait to get home. I realize I want to stop wandering myself. Knowing that the Barcelona postcard could have come from the gift shop feels like enough. I don't think I can face another European postmaster, or another day in the blinding sun.

The next day's travel home is a long, exhausted blur of checkouts and check-ins, tickets and airports, fruit juice and tiny foil snack packages. There is pressurized cabin air, a safety presentation, and hourly updates on the weather. In-flight magazines try to sell me on more vacations, and offer incredible inventions to put me at ease: cylindrical neck rests, earphone noise-reducers, easy-wrap garden hose storage units, suction-cup shower mirrors, ice-cube trays that make duck-shaped ice. It's all an effective distraction from the traveling that's actually happening.

By the time I drag my suitcase across the long-term parking lot and sit in my car, I am weary and ready to be done. I feel discombobulated, as if I've never even been in a car before, and now I'm sitting at the wheel, the inexperienced pilot of an amazing technological invention that will careen me down the highway at high speed.

I feel drunk.

Surprisingly, I quickly adapt to driving. The familiarity of the highways and exit signs puts me in a better state. Traffic seems to be flowing well, until I see a car pulled over on the right side of the highway with its hazards on. Everyone ahead of me taps their brakes to slow down and gawk instead of simply moving over to the left, as if they've never seen a car pulled over before.

"Don't stop on the highway," I say to the traffic, "just keep rolling."

Eventually the congestion clears, and I find my way onto more comfortable back roads away from all the noise. I think about my recent journeys and consider what I've found. London, Paris, and

Barcelona. Different people, language barriers, and blazing sun. Lots of strangers and unanswered questions. What kind of trip is that? What could Zoe have done there that would be so worth sending postcards about?

I open the window for some fresh air. The stars are out tonight, trying their best to shine through the haze of the spring humidity. Cassiopeia and the Big Dipper hang upside down in the sky. On the roadside ahead I spot a black-and-white animal. From my perspective, it looks like a miniature cow, but as I get closer, I see it's a cat with Holstein markings. The cow-cat sits on the edge of the road, ready to cross once I've passed. And I wonder, how can animals survive so close to speeding cars? I think of Zoe and her fierce compassion for animals, especially the feral and abandoned ones. She would probably make me pull over and feed it or take it to a shelter. But I keep on driving.

The night feels suddenly cold, and the stripes flow past my car in the same steady rhythm, like time slipping away. Dash dash dash. One by one.

I've read that in Haiti, magic is a part of ev-eryday life. Things happen because they do, and people know better than to try to explain it. Objects float against physical law and people know things they shouldn't. Zombies roam the earth. Many have witnessed the zombies, and reported them to be oddly familiar. They are not the glassy-eyed, open-mouthed, moaning creatures of horror movies, but everyday people caught in a half-animated state—quiet, desperate beings who swirl around in an eddy in the river of life. A curse, some say. A zombie curse. I've read several magazine articles on it, and I'm a believer.

It's a harder sell to my sister.

"You are not a zombie," Natalie says emphatically. Her effort to whisper in her office phone sounds like foamy-mouthed mad-ness. "You just got back from a nice cabin weekend away with friends. Aren't you supposed to be relaxed and refreshed?"

"There is a condition," I explain, "according to the Bizango secret societies, that is similar to a precancerous body state, only it's more of a primer for zombieness, or zombiehood, whatever you might call it."

Nat scoffs. "I wish I could go on a cabin weekend away with friends."

"Are you saying there isn't such a state?"

"No, there is certainly not," she hisses.

"A precancerous condition? Are you sure?"

"Yes, one can be in a precancerous condition, Sid, but you don't have cancer. We ran all those tests already, and your white blood cells are perfect. You don't even have signs of an infection. I'm sorry to say, but you are dangerously healthy."

I consider this, but MRIs and CATs and EKGs aren't designed to pick up pre-zombiehood conditions. Maybe there is such a machine somewhere in the dark heart of Haiti, but I'll need to do some more research.

"What about my genetic disposition for aneurysms?" I ask.

"What about it?"

"I could fall over tomorrow. Bam. Just like Mom."

"And I could get struck by a bus."

"But you're not walking around with a genetic disposition to walk in front of buses, Natalie. You don't walk in front of buses more than most people, putting yourself at greater risk than most people." I feel my voice rising against her whisper-scream defense. "I don't know that you even come in contact with buses, actually."

"I don't have time for this today."

"When is the last time a bus rolled through your waiting room? I mean, really, of course you're not going to get struck by one because the closest bus line is seven blocks from your office!" I loosen my grip on the phone, pull the hot receiver off my ear. I cool down while she mumbles something to her secretary.

"So what's your point," she says.

"Lousy metaphor."

"Point taken. No more bus metaphors."

"Don't get funny with me, doctor." She hates it when I call her doctor. "You know I'm right."

"You and I came from the same gene pool, *Sid*." I hate it when she says my name like that. "But there are no other family members with a history of aneurysm, and even if there were, the chance that you would develop the same thing Mom had is extremely low, due to your age alone. Just because Mom had an aneurysm doesn't mean you're going to have one. You may give me one, of course."

I pace in the living room, switch the phone to my cold ear. Nat's voice changes tone with the temperature. She sounds foreign, French maybe. I switch it back to the hot ear. I can't get over the feeling that there's something she's not telling me.

"We should feel lucky she went so fast," she says, "without any suffering."

"You're right."

"Mom was a rare case."

A rare case? That doesn't sound good. I've heard that all great medical students go through a period of time when they believe they have all or most of the symptoms of the diseases they study. Natalie never believed she had any disease. Maybe I'd make a great physician.

"Mom had a fusiform cerebral aneurysm . . ." she explains.

"Well, that makes it all clear."

". . . and that type of aneurysm rarely ruptures."

"If you say so," I say.

"What happened to Mom was a freak accident."

"Okay."

"Are we good for now?" she asks.

"Yes, I'll let you go then."

"Great. Thanks," she says, and hangs up.

Rare case, I think. Dangerously healthy. I rub my hot ear. The blood surges through my veins, over and around my eardrums. I listen closely for rare objects passing through my bloodstream: little freak accidents waiting to happen.

My watch seems to be ticking exceptionally loud, but it's only an acoustical trick. The kitchen clock, bedroom clock, and my watch will on occasion tick at the exact same time, causing a re-sounding knocking that echoes through the walls and my head. It's my telltale heart. And my heart says I'm late for some much-needed therapy.

The jets spray the bottom of my car with an impressive force. I drive slowly to allow the under-body a good rinse. I continue into the wheel guide; the tire drops in. The lights change from green to yellow to red, and the car tugs forward. A giant black robot arm comes alive, slides away from the wall and across the width of the car. The heart of the car wash pumps water and foam through the arteries along the robot arm until it can no longer take the pres-sure. Twenty-four valves simultaneously open and streams of soap shoot down across the hood. The first pass covers the left side with pink foam, and I'm already beginning to relax. I close my eyes and listen to the whirr-snap of the arm as it covers the rear window and makes its final turn to complete the first coat. Globs of foam slop over the windshield. Twenty seconds of pure bliss. I am relaxed and right with the world. Another coating will follow shortly, I know—the tri-color foam that acts as a cleaner and a shiner—but nothing can beat that first pink coat. I am to-tally entombed inside the car now, protected under a layer of candy froth, sheltered inside the cinder block building that rests beneath a swath of majestic maple trees.

This image is stuck in my mind: a glorious bloom of brain cancer squeezing my skull.

I sit in my dining room and try to focus on something tangible. Zero resting across the room. The smell of fresh-brewed coffee under my nose. It's not working. Usually the car wash trips help, but today this nagging picture overrides the peace of the pink foam.

Like kudzu tendrils slowly crushing an old Southern mansion, the disease's grip is slow and steady. And that wonderful and sickening lilac perfume lets me know it's there, doing its magic. Nothing personal, just hungry, need more room, don't I smell pretty?

I feel hot liquid scald my leg before I register the shattering sound. I've dropped my cup of coffee. I look down at the cracked mess—a broken relic at my feet, freshly left by someone other than myself, it seems. A clue to something, or a warning. People don't go just dropping things, the warning says. You're slipping, buddy. You are slip slidin' away.

"Believe we're gliding down the highway," I sing to myself.

Zero barks.

"You know the nearer your destination—"

He barks again.

"What!" I yell back.

Zero stops. He's not a barker, really. He's waiting for something. I lean down from my chair to pick up the pieces of the shattered coffee mug. He comes over and licks my face.

"All right, you've got my attention. So?"

Zero laps up the coffee on the floor.

"Hey, watch out, you might cut yourself. Coffee's not good for you anyway. No more coffee. I should take you to the vet one of these days."

He sits back and groans.

We sit in silence for a while. He lets out a shuddering sigh, like he knows I'm going to leave again but he's not sure for how long.

"Hey listen," I tell him, "I've got good news."

His ears perk up.

"I think I'm done with traveling for a while. I'm going to stick around."

I reach down and pat him on the head. He seems pleased.

"I just wonder if I've been looking in the wrong place all along," I say, and get up out of my chair.

The basement feels exceptionally musty tonight. Maybe it's just my mood. I feel like I need a Ouija board or candles and incense to get this going. I've never conjured Mom up before; she's always come to me. Although one might argue I've been conjuring her up this whole time.

I retrieve the dusty bottle of Bordeaux from underneath the stairs and set it up on the workbench. I clip a work lamp on a rafter and direct the light down at the bottle, interrogation-style. I look through the window well to see if any neighbors are watching, but only rocks and worms stare back at me. I pull up a chair and sit down.

"Mom," I say to the bottle. No response. I clap twice, like the Clapper. "Mom," I say louder. "It's Sid. We need to talk."

Again, no response, which is fine, I wasn't expecting the bottle would dance across the table. It doesn't really matter what level of poltergeist activity occurs. I need to say some things, so I start saying them. Maybe she's listening.

"My dog, Zero, is probably my best friend," I tell her. "He's a big help." I tell her how Natalie is pregnant now, and that she's turning into an angry, impatient version of her former self; I tell her about the red eye in the giant humming CAT-scan machine and the car washes.

I pause. Deep breath. I ask her if Zoe is on the other side and why she might be playing such a cruel game with the postcards. No answer.

"And why a bottle of French wine?" I ask, and stand up. "Why not a Californian or Australian?" I point at the bottle accusingly. "What happened to good old-fashioned mysterious phone calls? You know, static on the line? Spooky whispering?"

I must be getting pretty worked up because my heart starts to race and the scent of lilacs begins to float through the basement— a cloud of weighty perfume. I feel a chill in the air as the flowers fill my head. Mom pushes through then, a hushed voice, like I've awakened her from a nap.

"What are you saying?" she asks, her voice swirly and distant. "What are you saying to me?"

The work lamp suddenly glows brighter, infused with the new energy in the room. I squint under the hot light. My breathing labors, and I feel my balance washing out, my legs tingling, horizons tilting.

Her voice is loud, immediate, demanding: "What are you trying to say?!"

The room goes dark.

"Exhaustion," Dr. Singh says, avoiding eye contact. He dots *i*'s on his notepad, underlines a few words. He scribbles away, as if working out a complicated math problem, possibly constructing theorems that prove his patients aren't as important as he is. "You need rest," he concludes.

I don't care for the smell of this place—too much astringent and latex. "I collapse and all you can say is I need rest?"

Dr. Singh looks up briefly, about to explain himself, then continues writing. I'm not thrilled with his diagnosis, but I'm happy I managed to wake up unharmed in the basement and had enough sense to see my doctor without Natalie's assistance.

Dr. Singh finally takes a moment from his jotting. He studies me with an expression of gentle contempt. "The body gets its rest one way or another. You weren't giving it any, so it took it from you. Luckily, you weren't driving."

"What about my medical history?" I ask, and raise a finger to accentuate my point, but it has no effect. He dismisses my hypothesis with a quick head-shake.

"Your lab work is fine. But your electrolytes were probably down due to dehydration, and so you felt a lack of concentration, overwhelming tiredness." He touches his hands together, open-faced, giving me a gift, the answer to this simple problem: "Exhaustion." He plops down on a little four-wheeled stool to get on my level, and crosses his arms. "When is the last time you took a vacation?"

I open my mouth to explain about vacations and he cuts me off.

"Not a sightseeing vacation. That's work. I mean relaxing. Sitting on a beach for a week, sipping mai tais. Not worrying. Not working. Not exhausting yourself."

He puts extra emphasis on the word *exhausting*, perhaps so I'll realize that this word and my diagnosis might be somehow related. I decide not to tell him about my recent twenty-five-lap adventure through Soapy Sudz.

"Five days," he declares. "No work." He holds up his right hand and wiggles all five fingers. "Relax. Enjoy something. And it's best if you don't drink alcohol. Ignore my mai tai suggestion. Although when you're back in good health you might try a drink or two. I recommend red wine. It's great for your heart."

Suddenly Dr. Singh is caught up in a flurry of furious writing and violent *i*-dotting, the pen on the verge of ripping the paper. He fires off machine gun *t*-crossings, his brow furrowed hard. Deep creases cut into his forehead, subtle drops of moisture ride his lip. With an aggressive swoop-tap-tap and a loud rip, he hands me the yellow paper. "Remember, everything in moderation," he says, and quickly exits.

I look at the illegible mess of my prescription. It's strangely enticing. I know the only one who can read it is Candyce, the girl who sometimes works the front desk and is here today, but she may want to punch me in the stomach again after last month's incident.

chapter

31

The thing with Candyce wasn't entirely my
fault. The whole date, our dinner together,
it was really just a misunderstanding. I met
her at Dr. Singh's office before all this CAT-scan
business. I'd come after work to get a strange pain in my neck
checked out. She seemed so harmless sitting behind her desk,
answering calls with her velvet phone voice, dutifully marking
down appointments. She was so happy to be busy. I was feeling
pretty anxious about my neck, and this nice girl with a dyed blue
streak in her hair kept smiling at me between phone calls. And
it was soothing. So when I finished with Dr. Singh and got his
prescriptions, this same nice girl translated his handwriting for
me and answered all my questions about the medicine I'd been
prescribed, and assured me I'd be okay. I'd felt good about my
visit; she said I was going to be fine.

As I left the building, the sun was low in the sky. The end
of another day without Zoe. And then I heard footsteps sneak
up behind me and there was Candyce, smiling at me again. She
assured me one more time I'd be fine, and asked if I wanted to
get something to eat. And I was feeling so fine and assured that
I agreed without realizing I'd agreed, hadn't even thought about

it really, what all the implications might be. I was feeling good about my visit, and when she mentioned food, I realized that yes, I was hungry after being so worried all day. So I agreed to go to dinner. This was officially our first date, according to Candyce, or she wouldn't have been so upset, I'm sure of it.

As we walked downtown toward the restaurants, she started joking about how it was our first date and how romantic it was, then laughed at me and punched my shoulder when she saw my confused reaction, and we both laughed and it was all just a little uneven from the get-go.

We stopped at a sub shop. I thought this was a safe choice because to me, sub shop says *extremely casual dining*. She insisted on paying. I insisted we go Dutch. How cute, she said, our first date is Dutch, and then she laid on more of the romantic date business, making sure to roll her eyes so I knew she was kidding.

And we shared small talk, just the basics—if we liked our jobs, our favorite movies, the weather—and I could tell by the way she smiled that she liked me quite a bit, at least quite a bit more than I liked her. I mean, she's really sweet and cute, and like I said, she definitely put me at ease back at the doctor's office. She was very gracious. But then as we were sitting there and things seemed to be mellowing out, she gave me this strange look, like she might burst. She pressed her lips together so they formed a thin white line, and she started to look around as if something needed to exit her body and she needed a target. Then she looked directly at me. And sure enough, she opened her mouth and out came everything: a million words she could not stop.

As abrupt as it was, she managed to categorize most of it. First it was her general history: childhood highlights, family tree, education, dating history, hobbies, employment, and religion. Then it was random things: favorite colors, most embarrassing moments, fragmented dreams, philosophies on life. She spoke in such an urgent way, I'm not sure if she noticed I hadn't said a word. I did my best to listen.

She said things like:

"I used to like turquoise so much, because it's so blue, and green, together! But then I got seasick in Florida and now I like mauve."

And,

"People shouldn't lie, they should just be honest, because it saves so much time, and we totally don't have time to lie."

And,

"I have two brothers but they're both way older than me. I was an accident."

And,

"I almost died when I was four because I ate a bite of someone's peanut-butter-and-banana sandwich at school, and I'm allergic to peanuts. They had to call an ambulance and everything. "

And,

"I never understood that saying about how if a tree falls in the woods, does it make a noise?"

A tsunami of words. I had no idea it was coming, and it was much stronger and unrelenting than I ever could have expected. But after surviving the first wave, I knew there would be a second wave coming because she pulled out a box of Marlboros and started smoking with the hard exhale of someone who liked to talk while they smoked. I felt trapped, caught off-guard. I had no recourse, no protection.

So I ran.

Only to the restroom, but its tightly confined walls offered me some solace. I locked myself into a stall, enveloped in the silence of the tile floor, the white noise of the automatic flushing urinal system. It's where I stayed until I felt safe again. About twenty minutes later I came out and Candyce was gone. I felt relieved and terrible all at once. I stepped outside the sub shop's door and there she was, waiting for me on the sidewalk. "Are you feeling okay?" she asked.

"I think so," I said, and rubbed at my neck.

"Good," she said, and punched me square in the stomach. "Nothing's wrong with your neck anyway, you big baby." She turned on her heels, and stomped away, smoking and hissing.

Candyce is mostly a thoughtful girl, with a bit of a cruel streak when wronged. But that's okay because she can read Dr. Singh's handwriting and is willing to translate, and that is a gracious act in and of itself. Besides, she was right to punch me in the stomach. I should never have left her alone. I just panicked.

Sitting before me now, Candyce studies the cryptology of my prescription. Instead of immediately divulging the secret information, she chews on her lip. She looks at me, then back at the prescription, then up at me again. "It says you need to relax," she says finally. "No work for five days."

"Thanks," I say, and gesture toward the note. "Sometimes I don't understand simple things."

"I know."

I smile awkwardly.

"Hey! Let's go see a movie!" she says. "That'd be relaxing!" I start to form the words of a lie, but she cuts me off. "Pick me up here at seven," she says, and slaps the prescription in my hand.

Candyce is actually quite attractive. Aside from the blue streak down the middle of her black hair, she's got a great smile and pretty eyes. She's quirky and perky, which would be good if she were to take Dr. Singh's advice about moderation. There doesn't seem to be a cell of it in all of her attractive, quirky, perky body. Even in a terrifyingly public place like a movie theater.

"She was totally naked and fucking this guy next to me," she says, in a much higher pitch than she uses at the office. "And they weren't quiet about it either, I mean they're banging three feet away while I'm trying to sleep! And this is supposed to be my vacation! I'm like, shut the fuck up over there, you sluts!"

The movie theater is a classic 1920s movie palace, decorated in an ornate East Indian style. Hundreds of painted elephants parade across the walls. Some of them stare at me, wondering if Candyce will stop saying the word "fuck" while a family with young kids sits behind us, fully engaged by her blue-streaked hair and lack of moderation.

"Fucking unreal!" she screams, or at least it feels like it.

"Candyce," I whisper, smiling, trying to keep it light. "Please, for the children." I nod in their direction.

"So I ended up sleeping on the beach, for Christ's sake, on the beach! I spent all my money on a hotel room, and now I have a sore throat, and I'm sleeping on the beach because my roommate who is also supposed to be my friend can't stop—"

"Unbelievable!" I say. "That's not a good friend."

Candyce must sense my edginess because she sits back in her seat and stops talking. She studies me between sips of her giant soda and handfuls of my popcorn. I'm counting elephants: forty-seven so far.

"Can I ask you something?" she blurts.

"Shoot." I'm not sure I'm game, but it's an opportunity to re-direct her that I can't pass up. She offers me her soda first, and I surprise myself by sipping from her straw. She changes her position then, sits up a little more, attentive to my inevitable answer, honestly curious about how I'll respond. Five more elephants on the ceiling. Big ones. I'm surprised I didn't see them before.

"How did you get so exhausted?" she asks.

I stare at Candyce's hair, the shiny blue streak in particular. A unique hue swirls through it, almost metallic. Inside the blue stripe I see a distant memory of a deep bliss I once knew. It's buried inside a tomb of a room that is so full of something the door refuses to open. The house lights dim and I watch Candyce's eyes turn from blue to gray. She looks dead to me with her eyes agog, and she doesn't blink once until I look away.

Wanderlust Incorporated is busy today. The office noises blend together to create a frustrating soundtrack—soft enough so I can't hear the lyrics, but loud enough so I can't ignore the melody. What there is of it. Voices muttering sales pitches. Fingers tapping keyboards.

I sit upright in front of my computer and try to tune it all out. I've ignored Dr. Singh's prescription and come to work. Somehow it was easier than trying to explain to Steve that I need five days off to relax after my vacation. I watch The Randomizer pick a new number. The cursor blinks in time with the ringing in my headset.

A woman answers with a hello. She sounds nice, friendly. I listen to the dynamics of her voice, the subtle texture, the breathy timbre. She speaks again, more urgently: hello? I listen to her exhale. Is she really alive on the other side of the connection? What is she thinking about? Does it upset her that I'm reaching out to her only to be silent?

She hangs up.

The Randomizer dials again.

Steve left me a welcome-back gift. A nice gesture, albeit a

little odd. It's called a Bug-Out Bob. A little air-filled rubber guy whose eyes, ears, and tongue pop out when you squeeze him. A stress reliever, I suppose. Office gag. It sits on my desk, staring at me with fearful rubber eyes.

The ringing continues in my headset. I stand up to survey my workplace. Over the cubicle walls, I see nothing out of the ordinary. Steve is in his office. Workers are at the copy machine and fax. I sit back down.

A man answers this time. "Hello? Block residence."

I listen.

"Block residence? Hello?"

I say nothing, but grab the squeezie-doll and tighten my grip. "Who is this?"

I squeeze my fist hard. The doll's innards become outtards. I release.

"If you can hear me, say something."

Another squeeze. Eyes and ears and tongue bulge at impossible angles. I keep them bulging. The caller hangs up. I release and return Bug-Out Bob to his post.

I really should be responding to calls I've initiated today. To sell effectively, a certain amount of interaction is required. Interaction equals sales, and sales earn commissions, and commissions pay the bills—something I've been more than a little bit slack about lately. When Mom died, she left us with the house and the mortgage, and when Natalie moved out, I agreed to take it over. She's offered to help if I need it, of course, but I just can't ask her for any more help. Besides, the mortgage is now paid. It's just all those other bills. Well, at least the credit cards, as of late.

The Randomizer continues to dial. I study the postcards on my cubicle walls. What an odd invention, postcards. So unassuming. A little card with a place to write a note.

"Hello?" a voice asks.

Postcards, I want to say to the caller. One-way only. No return address. Who the hell came up with that anyway?

The caller hangs up without a challenge.

In order to feel productive, I begin to trap my scattered thoughts on Post-it notes. Somehow they feel safer confined to tiny yellow squares. They quickly accumulate, however, creating a pattern of chaos all of their own. Random statements and questions stuck to the table, one edge of each note lifting up and away as if desperately wanting to jump back in the fray.

- Pay bills
- Who invented postcards?
- Soft-sell, don't be pushy
- CAT scan
- Remember to Relax

I cover the loose ends with another note. And another. And another.

I know I shouldn't, but the credit card companies keep sending me offers, so I keep opening them. They're all so shiny and full of promise. The PlatinumExcella®. The PremierFreedom®. No annual fees. No interest for a year.

I already put my plane tickets on the DiamondPrestige®, and my hotel rooms on the TitaniumRewards®, which I think leaves a little room on my GoldPoints® card for a few other expenditures. I'm just trying to adhere to Dr. Singh's orders about taking some time off worrying.

In this spirit, I decide to blow off work today. And while I may be abusing my flex-time privileges to the max, Steve hasn't said anything, so I keep my focus on unwinding.

And what better place than the Arizona Day Spa? I've probably passed this place a hundred times on my way to Wanderlust, but never stopped before today. The sign outside is painted with saguaro cacti and a deep red sky. It seems like a place people would go to relax. I enter through the front door and into the lobby, which is all desert tones—peaches and browns and turquoise. The menu of treatments hangs above a faux adobe fireplace. The full-immersion mud bath is tempting, but I know I would feel guilty about the high price tag that goes along with it, hence kill-ing the whole effect. I also pass up the seaweed body-wrap and the chocolate face-painting for the wonderful dark heat of the cedar sauna, which is free with the daily entrance fee.

The smell of the sweet wood is intoxicating enough, but the heat is so delightfully stifling I almost forget my troubles. I sit and sweat and labor at breathing. I might be feeling happy; I'm not sure. I decide to sweat some more, let it drip off my eyelids. I've left the light off and it's the closest feeling I've had to the car wash that I can remember, so that's good. Then the door opens.

"Anyone in here?" a voice asks.

Damn it.

A click, and the room is filled with light.

"Oh sorry," the voice says. A forty-something man with an excess of body hair and a deep, orange-brown tan enters the sauna. He doesn't turn the light back off. "I love the sauna," he says, and pours a ladleful of water over the coals. Steam fills our little wooden box. The temperature increases. I forgive him for intruding; more steam is exactly what I needed. I feel like I'm breathing water now, or devolving to a single-celled creature made of pure liquid. A smoldering burn in my lungs forces me to breathe even slower. My eyes glaze over with sweat and I don't wipe it away.

The hairy orange man climbs up on the top level and stretches out the entire length of the bench—a sauna pro. Oranga-man, I think, I am in a sauna with a large monkey. He gives a quick ex-halation to acknowledge my presence—or a grunt to ward off the other monkeys in the rain forest. "Good for the soul," he says. "Sweats out the demons."

I grunt back, and think about demons seeping out of my pores—little imps melting and running down the tip of my nose, absorbing into the cedar planks below. And although I can barely breathe, all I want is for this stranger to be replaced by someone female, and I want to be sweating with her, mixing our demons together, sliding across each other's skin, breathing each other's hot breath, feeling the smoldering burn, until we both turn to liquid and evaporate.

"You look a little peaked, friend," the orange man says. "You didn't fall asleep in here did you?"

I force myself to sit up, and sure enough my head begins to spin.

"Too much of a good thing can be bad, you know," he says. "Everything in moderation."

My cell phone vibrates just as Gazelle has completely encased me in a tub full of black, mineral-enriched, Moor peat mud. I set the phone to vibrate in consideration of my fellow entombed ones. I look down the row of the other graves-ites adjacent my own, the pasty faces poking up from the ground, ceremonial cucumber slices covering the eyes of the dead. If they notice the buzzing, they're not letting on.

I considered leaving my phone in the locker room, but I'm still waiting for that call about the CAT-scan results. Now I'm not sure I can even answer because I can barely move my arms against the weight of the heavy earth. I'm covered in too much of a good thing. It's okay, though. I won't worry about it: doctor's orders.

My phone rests atop a clean, white, folded towel next to the mud bath, as if it's on its own separate spa retreat. I glance at the number. It's a 201 area code. New Jersey. I manage to slip my arm out, clean my hand on the towel, and answer before it stops buzzing.

"I found out more about you and your girlfriend," the man says on the other end of the line. It's Corey, the reluctant clerk from Sunny Smiles. Hearing him say the word *girlfriend* feels unfamiliar and somewhat scary; I try to place its meaning and context, but it's got my head spinning. I pull myself up out of the ground, slowly, my ear tight to the phone. "To be honest with you," he says, and then he tells me what he knows, that when he put my cell phone number in his computer, it showed that my girlfriend and I were there about a year ago. "What was her name again?" he asks.

"Zoe?" I answer in a question. Her name sounds so strange out loud. Hollow, yet hopeful at the same time. Something inside me snaps to attention.

"You had a problem with your suspension, some kind of CV boot situation."

"What's a CV boot?"

"Has to do with the integrity of the front axle."

"Huh."

"That's what the records show anyway."

I feel my heart sink from the pressure of phantom thoughts, bits and pieces of truths not quite ready to be known—it's a weight heavier than forty feet of mud. I stop breathing for a moment, then inhale suddenly, a cartoon gasp. Corey tries to explain in between the dropouts of my cell connection, but I'm not listening anymore. In the spa windows I see my reflection: a pale white gangly mess, chunks of earth sliding down my body. I am alive from the grave.

"One of the guys said she spoke in a foreign accent sometimes. Chinese, maybe?"

The satellites in the heavens must be shifting because Corey's voice goes distant and fuzzy, then drops out completely.

Gazelle approaches me with a glass of water. "It's better if you stay covered for the full treatment," she says. "You should get back down there."

No thanks, I say internally, but I feel my head nodding yes, yes.

Yes, Gazelle, yes.

chapter

36

The voice isn't familiar, but the number is. It's the collection service.

"Sid's not here," I say into my cell, and look out at the vastness of my dark backyard. I prop myself against my shovel. Digging is hard work, but I realize I might have the beginning of something wonderful: a six-foot-by-three-foot hole, almost a full twelve inches deep. The stranger continues to talk anyway—a real collection whiz—but I'm distracted with noticing how incredibly vibrant my skin feels since visiting the Arizona Day Spa. I've been going daily for two weeks now. It's like my epidermis is vibrating.

The collectors have all tried different ways to fool me. Yesterday an older, assertive woman insisted I call her back as soon as possible about important information concerning my account. I enjoyed her performance; it was bold and brassy. She put a little street into it, got a little tough. The day before that, a guy with a Bible belt accent and damnation in his voice warned me of repercussions. He used that word a lot: repercussions. I remember hearing about percussion bombs in the news and thinking how they must be loud and violent and obtrusive. So repercussions must be especially bad. The guy who's on the phone now is real nice and friendly, like he's my favorite uncle, Ricky, calling to take me out to a ballgame.

"So, pal, how's it going today?" he asks.

"Pretty good, buddy," I return, just as sweet.

"Sid?"

"Sid should be back later. He's at work."

"He must work a long shift. He was just at work twelve hours ago."

"Yeah, he works funny shifts. A hard worker, that one."

"I'm talking to Sid, aren't I?" he says, silky smooth.

"Nope. Sid will be back later."

"Come on, Sid. We need you to make a payment. It's the responsible thing to do. You've exceeded your limit."

"I'll have him call you tomorrow."

"Be a man, Sid—"

I hang up the phone, unearth my shovel, and slice back into the ground with its tip. It's a good night for digging. Cool. Serene. I can almost feel the night birds watching me. Another two feet and I will have my very own mud bath. I'll never need to pay the Arizona Day Spa again. And the cost of a tip for water, towels, and fruit service can get expensive, which the collectors sometimes take the time to mention while going over my current balance due. If they freeze my cards, that's fine, I don't need them anymore. And if the phone company wants to turn my phone off, that's okay too. They never give good service anyway.

I decide it's time for a test. What the hell. It's no therapy-grade peat mud, but it will do. I toss in a few dozen spadefuls of loose dirt, roll out the garden hose, turn on the water, and let it flow into the hole. I watch the sky as I wait. The dark shadow of an owl glides silently overhead. Maybe I'm being visited by my spirit animal as I live this secret, nocturnal life: my predatory backyard existence. I try to spot the owl's location in the trees but something else catches my eye. It's Mary Jo, at the edge of my property.

"What are you doing?" she asks. She stands there, staring through the dark at the hole in my yard.

"Just digging in the dirt," I say. "What are *you* doing?"

She creeps closer to get a better look. Something about my answer doesn't sit well with her. She looks at my shovel, then at me. "My folks are playing cards next door. What are you making?"

"Well," I say, "it's sort of a project, I guess."

Her eyes are wide and luminous, held steady on the dark puddle of water. She sighs. "I can't swim."

"Oh, it's not for swimming."

She waits for me to explain, but when I don't, she blurts, "It looks like a grave."

I laugh a little, then take a good look at the hole. Sure enough, it does look that way. "You're right," I say, without thinking.

"Are you digging a grave?"

"No," I say quickly.

She backs up a few steps. "When my grandpa died, they put him in a hole like that. Are you gonna bury someone?"

"Oh, no. Of course not. It's not a grave."

"Did someone die?"

"No," I assure her. "It's not what you think—"

She keeps backing up, her voice rising. "Did you kill someone?"

I reach my hand out to stop her. "No! It's a spa, okay? It's a mud bath!"

She looks cautiously at the hole again. "Killing is a sin," she warns, continuing her slow escape.

"It's a mud bath," I say. "For relaxing. Grown-ups sit in mud to relax!"

She squints at me. "No they don't. My parents don't."

"Well, some do."

"You're lying. People don't sit in mud."

"Sure they do."

She looks terrified. I decide some levity might ease her fears. I jump in the hole. "See?" I splash around, toss some mud in the air for added effect. "It's fun!"

She stares at me, aghast. A loud clucking noise escapes her throat, and she unintentionally jumps straight up in the air. She lands, spins around, and dashes toward the black edge of my yard, the soles of her feet white flashes in the night.

I want to yell more assurances to her, but she's gone. Oh well. She'll keep my little secret; it's her secret now too. I lay back and try to enjoy my new creation. The mud's consistency is all wrong, though, and the water is way too cold. It's downright freezing. I hear shuffling in the far reaches of the yard and wonder if Mary Jo has returned in a more jovial mood, but soon Zero comes up to the edge. When he sees me, he lets out a big sigh and lies down.

"It's a spa," I tell him. "For relaxing."

He doesn't have anything to add, so we sit there for a while together, under the silence of the starry night.

The next morning, I am restless. I stand before the kitchen window, cereal bowl in hand, shoveling wheat flakes in my mouth. I chomp and slurp while staring at the apparent grave I've dug in the backyard. I finish eating, toss my empty bowl in the sink, and wonder what to do with myself.

Instinctively, I grab the phone to dial Natalie. Her number makes the shape of a house with half of a roof. I punch the speed dial instead and hit send. Maybe I can get some answers out of her about my CAT scan. The musical beep-boops sing out like so many other speed-dial songs—for all I know it's all the same song, put there to let me know everything is working.

I heard somewhere that soda machines actually had to be rebuilt by engineers because they were too quiet. People would put their money in the machine, press a selection, and somewhere between the selection pressing and the five seconds it took to drop the correct beverage, the customer would lose his temper and kick the shit out of the machine. Five seconds. Too many machines were being destroyed, so the engineers redesigned them to include loud clicks and buzzes and a tumbling drop to fill in the silence.

The problem with my cell phone isn't that it's too quiet, it's just inconsistent. Somehow my house is stuck between the analog tower and the digital tower. Every two minutes my connection changes. Analog, digital, roam. One bar, four bars, no service. It seems random when I'm talking, but there's a pattern, I'm sure of it. Like someone turning a switch in the Great Cell Phone Lab, and I'm the rat experiment. How many clicks will make the rat throw the phone against the wall?

Natalie picks up, but I can't hear her voice.

"It's your brother!" I yell, as if by sheer volume I will transmit a better signal. Natalie has had it with my shoddy coverage, and I keep telling her I'm going to throw my phone out the window one day. She tells me I always say that.

"Sid? Is that you?" *Ksssh.*

"It's me. Can you hear me?" *Ksssh. Ksssh.* "Nat?"

"Yeah, I can hear you. What's up?"

"There you are."

"When are you going to get a new phone?" she asks.

"Tomorrow. I promise."

Another click. More static. Silence.

Dial tone.

I press speed-dial number two. *Beep boop boop*, it sings. *Boop boop beep*. She picks up.

"Make it quick, Sid."

"Sorry. I'm really going to throw this out the window one day. Seriously."

"Promises, promises."

"I wanted to know if you heard back about the CAT scan. I know it takes a while, but—"

Kshhh. Click.

"Hello?"

Beep boop boop, boop boop beep. Another voice. "Hello, Dr. *Kssssh*'s office."

"Natalie?"

"*Kssssh* is with a patient right now."

"Linda, it's me, Sid." Linda is Natalie's office manager, and she doesn't like me because I often refer to her as *the secretary*. She is not the secretary, she has pointed out, she is *the office manager*, and she could use a secretary herself. "Can I please talk to Nat?"

"She just ran down the hall. She's really busy today."

"Can you just ask her—"

Analog. Digital. Roam.

"Hello?" Linda's voice does a herky-jerky dance. "What did you say?"

I shout through the waves of static. "Tell her to call me back!"

Dial tone. No signal.

When I throw the phone against the wall, it hits with a loud crack, but to my dismay, it doesn't shatter into a million pieces— not even a few dozen. It's only scratched on one side. I flip it open and look at the screen.

Four bars.

I stare at my damaged phone, and wait for my heart to stop beating so fast. The coverage bars pulse up and down like the decibel meter on a stereo system, and I get lost in the rhythm of a memory. It's one I haven't had in a while. In it, I'm lying in a gurney.

"Do you know where you are?" the voice asked. I could hear intercoms above me and clattering wheels below me. I was strapped to the gurney. The controlled urgency of a woman's voice felt like the way a nurse speaks, and I was putting it all together when she said it: "You're at a hospital." Judging by the speed of the passing lights above, I guessed this was also an emergency. I was right. "There's been an accident. You're being taken down to trauma right now. It's important that you lie still."

Square after square of ceiling tile passed above me, every few beats a flash of blinding white light. All I could think about was where the dog went. I must have kicked or flinched at one of the flashes because the nurse reached around to tighten down the straps across my legs. I wanted her to tie down my arms and my torso too, so I could never leave the gravity of the cart. I was afraid I might fly off and float into the sky. And I couldn't stop wondering where my dog went, which was strange because I knew neither Zoe nor I owned one. I wondered if Zoe was around, but somehow knew she wasn't, so I didn't ask.

A vague block of time passed, with various fussing and explanations. Most of it happened under bright lights. Strangers' heads floated in and out of my field of vision. Flashes of hot and cold and relief and pressure happened at unannounced intervals, and finally I made it to my resting room. It was quiet there, and dark—such a relief, the lack of light—like a cool bath after a day in the desert. They'd wrapped my head in gauze, so I could only see from my left eye, and something must have gone wrong with my mouth because I had a rubber piece across my teeth and packing under my lips.

My shift nurse arrived. A sturdy blond woman in her forties, she had especially meaty forearms. Her motions felt rehearsed: she draped an extra blanket across my body, tutored me on the emergency call button, pointed out the location of the bath-room. She spoke in a singsong way that she might have assumed was soothing and carefree, but was actually difficult to follow. It quickly became aggravating.

As she rolled the Venetian blinds open, slats of pink sliced across her uniform. She looked like a giant candy cane. "What a wonderful sunset," she sang, and gestured for me to take a look. But my one good eye was blind with pink and all I could do was shut it tight to keep out the burning. "So wonderful, sunsets," she hummed to herself. "Would you like this kept open?"

"No," I grunted through the packing and the dried blood and the rubber, then thought, Close the damn blinds.

"I'll leave them open for you," she whispered, and exited the room.

Days later, my good eye worsened and the doctor rolled gauze across that too.

Natalie eventually came to visit. I could hear her voice in the room, but through the bandages she was only a vague form with blurry appendages moving around as she spoke. "We'll make it through this," the blob said, "just like we always do."

She was right; we did make it through. Ten days later, we drove home and continued to breathe and eat and sleep and work. But I think part of both of us also didn't make it through. A couple of months after my accident, Natalie moved out to live with her boyfriend Jake, and I was left to live in our childhood home by myself. She abandoned the part of her that didn't make it through and started a new life as a hardworking physician, wife, and soon-to-be mother. And the part of me that didn't make it through, well, I guess I was still looking for that.

The four bars on my phone are holding
steady, finally, while my hands are anything but. I push speed-dial, but acciden-
tally hit the wrong number. I slap it shut and
open it again. The coverage bars flicker. I dial the half-house
shape.

"Thank you for calling Oak Valley Medical," the recording
says. "All of our lines are busy right now, but we will get to you as
soon as we can."

Linda once pointed out that their office phone system doesn't
allow them to see incoming numbers. So now I know the lines
really are busy. I'm not being ignored, I'm just in line with
everyone else who's trying to get hold of Natalie or one of
the other eight physicians who share the office with her. So I
should be feeling patient. All I need is thirty seconds. I just want
to know what the CAT-scan results say. I just want a reason for
the lilacs in my head—even though deep down, under the pink
car-wash foam, the black-and-white cat, the visions of orange
sunsets, and my blue Zoe bliss, I'm pretty sure I know the
reason.

"There are four calls ahead of you," the recording says.

The lilac swell is back; I have to lie down. I walk to my bed-room and stretch out on the bed, and listen to the orchestral Muzak pipe through the phone. The music reminds me of old-time silent movies, the kind my mom used to watch.

The lilac bushes were in the back, a long line of them that made up the property boundary. They'd grown high, about seven or eight feet, and those two weeks in May when they bloomed, it was really something. The air was heady with sweetness. You couldn't help but breathe deeper and more often to keep that scent in your head.

Mom and I were out cutting off clumps of lilac to put inside the house and we were doing this deep breathing to smell everything, and we both got a little light-headed, I think, because we weren't talking as much and she started laughing, which made me start to laugh, and soon we were laughing at our laughing, which led to more, and I remember reading somewhere that what the devil hates most is when families laugh together because that means they are full of love and hope and joy. And I thought, boy, Satan must be pissed right now, which made me laugh even harder. Finally we wound down and kept clipping lilacs, and I remember feeling a little dizzy. Once I got my head back, I looked over and saw Mom lying in the grass. "Mom?" I asked, and leaned down to her. "Mom, are you all right?" I asked as she lay still in the grass, staring up at the sky.

Rivulets of blood. That's what I remember thinking. A spy novel I read once described the heroine's gunshot wound this way, as it bled across her alabaster skin: tiny rivulets of blood. It was almost magical. But in real life, it just looked like a straight line of bright red color, plain and simple, from her nose to her cheek to the ground. I was afraid to touch her.

"Mom?" I asked again.

chapter

41

The orchestra music stops abruptly, followed by a few seconds of silence. I stand up to more actively wait for Linda or Natalie or anybody to answer. The coverage bars teeter and sway.

"There are two callers ahead of you," the recording tells me in a cheery voice. The violins and cellos continue.

"Damn it," I mutter, and kick the air. I come to my senses and realize I could've used the house phone line and avoided all this hassle, which only makes me more upset. But there is no way I'm hanging up now. "No way," I say to myself in the dresser mirror, and give the dresser a little push with my foot.

I remember being in the hospital with Natalie when we found out Mom was never coming back. The two of us sat at a waiting-room table adjacent a window. Nat had just verbalized the reality of our new life without Mom, said something like "She's not coming back" or something more obvious, like "Mom is dead." I don't remember the exact words because as she was saying them, the sun rose above the horizon, and that awkward first light of day filled the room with a heavy, yellow haze. Like something out of the movies. It bothered me when it happened like that, like a manufactured scene. The new light as our old lives had passed. On to the next chapter in the book of life. That kind of shit. I just wanted to go home and sleep. We'd been there for hours and I knew she was dead the moment she dropped in front of the lilac bushes. All of this waiting around was for nothing.

"You are the next caller," the recording cheers. "Someone should be with you shortly. Thank you for calling Oak Valley Medical." The music drops out, followed by a series of queer electronic noises. I imagine an old-school switchboard operator weeding her way through a wall of impossibly tangled cords, searching for mine with one hand, unplugging someone else's with another. I stare into space, waiting for my connection. The odd sounds continue, and then something more familiar.

Click.

Ksssh.

Dial tone.

"No," I mutter, and start to smile. The absurdity of this is funny. But I'm not feeling funny, and I look up at the dresser mirror and find a way to express how I am feeling. My fist lights up in a blossom of pain. The shattering sound is exactly what I need.

I watch the tanks to keep my mind off the needle in my hand. Memorial Hospital was a good choice because it offers a wonderful distraction with its cable television, but round-the-clock coverage of the war is not helping my woozy stomach. Not to mention that the intern working me over can't be more than twelve years old. I know he needs to learn suturing sometime, but I'd prefer that it wasn't on my hand on this morning. The pressure of the needle is quickly replaced with a painless, tingling sensation, for which I'm grateful.

The doctor never told me his name, so I'll call him Chip. Chip is busy preparing instruments on his surgical tray: bright, metallic objects that smell of steel and alcohol. I can't watch.

I'm at Memorial instead of Oak Valley because showing up at Oak Valley with my hand bleeding would've been the perfect reason for Natalie to call a Section Eight on me. "I don't get it, so you were mad at your phone?" she would've asked. Linda would've rolled her eyes. Better that Natalie not know about it, so here I am.

Channel 42 is doing its best to entertain with highlights of a recent desert battle. Angry men in robes launch a makeshift artillery round from one mountain to another. It explodes out of the barrel with ferocious velocity, screaming through the hot air. Moments later a puff of smoke flashes in the distance, a disappointing finish to them, as it inflicts no damage to the unseen enemy. The rebels seem tired with their latest attack. They rest behind a sandbag bunker and smoke cigarettes.

Chip tugs on my hand. He must be confusing the fine art of sutures with the yarn-loop picture he got from Grandma last Christmas.

"Easy, tiger," I say.

Peripherally, I see him stealing glances to monitor my agitation level. He takes a deep breath and goes back in, just as a soldier on TV swings a metal detector across a sandy road. He gingerly steps forward and swings again. He does this swinging and stepping in all directions, his dog by his side.

"One more to go," the boy-doctor ventures.

I hear the snip of his scissors. My face blanches. I try to swallow. My mouth is an arid wasteland. The mountain soldier drops another mortar round, steps back, and plugs his ears.

"Quite a fall you took," Chip says.

Shut up and stitch, I say, but realize I'm only thinking it. He does the agitation check again and I feel the last tug, which is good timing because the battle is over and now there is only footage of anchor-desk reporters laughing at their own jokes, cracking themselves up, filling time until the producers say enough.

The Vicodin I've been prescribed has left me feeling soft and fuzzy. I've taken to napping on the living room couch. A voice breaks through my happy haze, distant and harsh, a police cruiser radio in miniature. "Sid," it says, "I heard a rumor you're hitting mirrors again. Over." I lift my head off the cushion, and half-wait for a tiny squad car to shoot across the living room like the chuck wagon in those old dog-food commercials. "Call me back to confirm. It's your sister." I scramble off the couch and grab the receiver.

"Hey."

"Oh you are there," she says. "I was just leaving a message."

"Yeah, I'm here."

"So? What's this about hospital treatment? Are you all right?"

"Who told you that?" I ask, and look at my freshly bandaged hand. It still hurts if I clench my fist tight enough. "That's crazy talk."

"I have my connections."

"Hypothetically, if I did get hospital care, wouldn't that be a violation of patient privacy rights to share that information?"

"My old secretary Estelle told me she saw you in the waiting room. I put the rest together on my own."

"Estelle, huh? You sure she's not your old office manager?"

"What?"

"Big difference between secretaries and office managers. Ask Linda."

"So you did it again," she says, expertly dodging my dodge.

Zero stands by the picture window, staring out at something in a tree.

"Animal attack," I say.

"Mm-hm."

"Rabid squirrels. It happens."

"More jokes. That's good. Listen, I know you don't want to hear this, but I think you should see someone about your anger problem."

"You think I'm angry?" I couldn't be feeling more relaxed and content. Maybe it's the pills.

"People don't punch mirrors because they feel breezy."

"Who said I punched a mirror?"

"I'm not saying you need a shrink, Sid. I just think you need to relax. My friend Myna has a yoga class. You should check it out."

"Is she a bird?"

"What?"

"Never mind."

"They meet on Saturday afternoons at the top of Cherry Hill, overlooking the lake. You breathe, stretch, relax. How about I tell her you might be coming?"

I really don't have an excuse to avoid this one. I think I will take up her offer. How hard can breathing and sitting be? "Sure," I say.

"I really think you should do this," she argues. "I don't know what else to say."

"I said yes. I'll go."

"Really?"

"Yeah, why not."

"I'm so glad to hear you say that."

I can tell she is consciously keeping her scolding tone at bay for now. I have made a breakthrough and Dr. Nat is pleased.

"I think you'll like it," she continues to coax. "Let me know how it goes."

"You bet," I say, and hang up before I can take it back. I'm so tempted to write this off as Nat's last-ditch effort before she decides to call an interventionist, but I actually feel pleased with the idea now that I've committed to it. Maybe some oxygen and Cherry Hill breathing is just what I need. If the mud and the car washes don't work, maybe there's something better up on the hill waiting for me. Or maybe it's the pain killers talking.

Sit and breathe. This is what we do on top
of Cherry Hill. All twenty of us, in loose
rows of five, facing the instructor. We all sit
on thin blue mats, stare out at the lake on a beautiful Saturday, and breathe.

At first it's difficult because I'm terribly distracted. A girl
on the hill seems familiar to me, and I can't stop staring at her.
Her hair is long and chocolate-brown, simply cut, plain. She's a
beautiful stranger.

I name her Jane.

Jane sees me watching her but doesn't seem to mind. It's like
she can sense my apprehension and knows it will dissipate once
I surrender to the sitting-and-breathing groove. I close my eyes
and fake contentment, but I can't seem to keep my balance, even
though I'm only sitting. Who ever had difficulty with sitting?

Keeping my eyes closed helps. I can't see anyone's reaction to
my insecurity. I remember why this was so effective when I was a
child, the magical curtain of invisibility. But I don't want to disappear; I want Jane to know I'm here.

I open my eyes again and search the sky. Clouds build in vast
piles like something out of a John Ford film—a towering anvil

bulging upward as it reaches for the stratosphere. Myna reminds us to inhale and exhale, which is good because I've almost forgotten to breathe.

I notice how my shoulders slump down as I stare upward—not exactly the lotus-blossom position. I straighten up and catch Jane glance and exhale through a grin. She pretends not to notice me noticing her notice. It's suddenly become very complicated, and my mind can't stop spinning with the infinite amount of possible outcomes due to this Jane girl breathing and sitting on a mat two rows over on top of a cloud-ridden Cherry Hill. We're supposed to be thinking of nothing and I'm busy with everything: should I smile back, should I say hello later, do I cause harm by thinking these thoughts, do I cause harm by believing there is something else out there, could it be a lunch date, would we have any commonalities, can I stop searching for the source of lost love, is that fair to Zoe, is that fair to Candyce, is that fair to Jane? Does she know what she's getting into by glancing at me, and when does it all really begin, and does it ever end?

The instructor strikes a small gong with a soft mallet. The sound is gentle but firm and all the other sitter-breathers look so calm, luminescent even, highly-evolved tranquil balls of shimmering light. I think I've drawn blood on the inside of my cheek from chewing so hard.

"Thank you all for coming," the instructor says, her voice so soft and warm.

I cough.

"Let's remember," she says. "Don't be bad. Don't be good. Just be."

Just be, I think, just be. It's agonizing. Jane seems to have no problem just being. She has beautiful eyes, even when they're closed. The balls of light let out a collective happy humming sound, vibrate off their mats, and float to their body-transportation devices.

Jane rolls up her mat and pretends not to notice me noticing her. She takes a few pulls from her purple water-bottle and with great purpose begins her stroll down the side of Cherry Hill. And here I sit, just being.

"Are you Sid?" Myna asks, gracefully tossing her tote bag across her shoulder. We are the only two left. "Natalie's brother, right? I'm Myna."

"Hello Myna. Yes, I'm Dr. Nat's brother." Jane is out of reach now, a dangerously safe distance away.

"She said you'd be coming. What'd you think?"

"It was really relaxing," I say, and my tongue finds the crater in my cheek. Tastes like copper. "Peaceful."

"You came on a great day," she says. "You should come back next week. We'll be here." She points to the horizon over the lake. "Don't stay too long. You might get wet."

I scramble to my feet and wave good-bye. "Thanks," I say. Far in the distance, the monster anvil cloud has become ominously dark, spreading with great determination. Fat cloud tumors burst forth in a frenzy of malevolent growth, and yet not a drop of rain nor howl of wind. But something is most certainly up there, brewing, waiting, being.

Back home, I sit on my front porch and stare at the mailbox. Mary Jo is out in her yard doing cartwheels, laughing, singing, enjoying this lovely day with wild abandon. She doesn't seem to mind the storm cloud on the horizon. She's focused on the sunny part of the day. I pretend to enjoy it as well. I smile up at the sun, imbibe the summer air. I can taste the rain even though it hasn't fallen.

What I'm really doing is waiting for the mailman. I'm waiting for him to come poking along in his blue-and-white Jeep, waiting for the way he leans out the wrong side of the car, his thumb covered with a little knobby rubber tip as he flips through envelopes like a Vegas blackjack dealer, sliding the mail into the box with a snap so it hits the back with a low-pitched *pang*. I listen for the intermittent revving of the Jeep's engine.

He usually drives by at 4:45, which seems late in the day for mail delivery. I used to deliver newspapers in the predawn hours, and my reward for finishing my route was sunlight, knowing I could go home and sleep until noon. But this guy, he's coming after 4:30. Some days it's as early as 3:30, but once it was almost 4:55, which makes me itchy with panic. Who delivers this late in the day? And how did we get on the late schedule? Doesn't the post office work like the army? "Getting more done by nine a.m. than most people do all day," like in their recruitment commercial? I can't take this waiting, especially on a Saturday.

What's sick is I don't even want these postcards, but since they started arriving I can't wait for the next one. It's been a while since the Barcelona card and I'm wondering if any more are on their way. Maybe a stranger's hands are holding my fate right this second, large, hairy hands sifting through a bulging burlap bag. Or maybe there's some big European guy loading a sack of mail into the belly of a plane, and saluting the pilot as the jet taxis down the tarmac. Maybe that bag of mail is flying over an ocean right now, on its way here above turquoise waters to entice me toward another fabulous destination.

I sit on the porch in this eager state. My stomach feels hollowed out by the sheer ache for new contact. I want to gather the postcards and present them to Zoe one day in the future so we can have a laugh together about how I used to sit on the porch steps day after day like a child waiting for the ice cream man.

My thoughts are interrupted by that wonderfully familiar sound: the intermittent revving, the slight squeak of front disc brakes, the low-pitched *dong* like a winner's bell at the circus. He is coming.

Mary Jo stops her cartwheeling and is now attached to her mailbox. She must have heard the same sounds I did. She shows no fear of me today, as if the sunshine erased all traumatic memories of her dark backyard encounter with my pseudo-grave.

"What'd you do to your hand?" she shouts, ever the inquisitor.

I forgot about my bandage and hold it out as if it's the first time I've seen it, this altered hand.

"Oh, it's nothing," I say. "I fell."

"In your mud bath?"

"So now you believe me."

"My dad told me that some people do sit in mud to relax. He said that he likes to polish his sports car to relax. It's black, see?" She points to their driveway, where an ebony Porsche sits dormant. "He said he likes to make it look like nighttime, so it's like a shadow."

"Wow. That sure is black," I say, and turn to see the blue-and-white Jeep as it revs up to my neighbor's mailbox and pauses. The mailman rifles through his deck.

"Is your mud hole like a shadow?" she asks.

"I don't know."

"Are you married?" she asks.

I give her my best that's-an-adult-question look, but she's not getting it. "No."

"Do you have a girlfriend?"

I think about that. "No," I say.

"Why not?"

"I just don't."

She barely pauses before she's got another question. "Are you lonely?"

I watch the postal truck. The driver does something with a rubber band and a stack of envelopes, and then the Jeep surges forward.

"Are you?" she asks.

"What?"

"Are you lonely? Without a girlfriend?"

The truck drives right past my driveway, not even a friendly nod from the driver. No postcards today. I feel a new hole in my stomach begin to open.

Mary Jo stares at me from the other side of the street, waiting for an answer.

"What about you," I ask, a little peeved, "always playing in the yard by yourself? Aren't little kids supposed to have friends or something? Aren't *you* lonely?"

She frowns a little, looks at her feet, spins around in a full circle. "So, you don't know any girls?" she probes. "Not any?"

What is wrong with me, taking out my frustration on a ten-year-old. I think about her question, really think about it, then offer her a real answer in a real, here's-a-serious-answer voice. "Well, there is—" I start, but before I can finish explaining, she gallops across her yard. She stops in front of her dad's black Porsche and stares into the inky finish for a moment, like she's under a spell, then runs inside.

"There is one girl," I say to her empty yard.

Dream interpretation has never made sense to me, but Candyce seems to be handling it masterfully. She's dressed only in underwear and a T-shirt, stretched out before me on my bed, lying on her belly, her feet doing little swim-kicks in the air. "And so you were there in my dream, but it wasn't *you*-you, and we were at my house, but it wasn't my *house*-house, you know what I mean?" She searches my eyes for any comprehension. "Like instead of being a one-story ranch house in the Midwest, it was a tin shack in the Everglades, and it was upside down, and it didn't have any windows, but it was still my house, you know? Like I could *feel* it was my house."

"Right."

"And you were there, but weren't really *you*-you."

"Uh-huh."

"Instead of being a thin white guy, you were, like, a giraffe."

"Wow."

"And you were blue, with three heads, and you didn't have any faces. But I knew it was you."

"Wow," I say again.

"Yeah," she says, and flips over on her back. She takes a long drag off her cigarette, and stares through the ceiling, deep into another dimension. She sits up then, a little more intense than before, and pulls herself closer to me. "And then, I'm remembering this now as we're talking, then we were having sex, but it wasn't *sex*-sex, like normal, because I was like a small brown dog, and you were a cloud, hovering over me in the yard, raining your seed in my fur." Her eyes are urgent, anticipative.

"That's pretty wild."

"Isn't it?" She opens her mouth, lets her chin hang in exasperation. We nod at each other a few times.

"I had a dream last night," I say, surprised that I'm sharing.

Candyce taps her cigarette into a makeshift aluminum foil ashtray. "Do tell."

"I was standing outside a bus looking in through its open doors, and all I could see was blackness, like a totally black cave."

"What happened?"

"That's it."

Candyce pouts. "That's all?"

"Yeah, that's all I remember."

"That's so sad," she says.

"Why?"

"You're depressed."

"Because of a bus?"

"The bus obviously symbolizes your travels through life, and the darkness means you feel those travels are empty and meaningless. I mean, that's pretty textbook."

"Actually, my neighbor has a black car, I was probably just dreaming of that."

"Okay, sure. If that's what you think." She lies back, staring at the ceiling. "What did you cut your hand on?" she asks.

"He really does have a black car. It's really, really black."

"Cool," she says, and crushes out her cigarette. Then she works her way over to me, snuggling close, tucking her head in my armpit. "Can we just lie here for a while?"

"Sure, that's fine," I say, and wonder how I got this half-naked girl in my bed next to me. She smells good. She rustles around, and I feel the stirrings of something human again. Something about her lying next to me clears my mind. I rest my head on hers and breathe in her blue hair, and soon enough I slip into my dreams.

Jane doesn't scream as she slides down the length of rope. She tightens her grip, silently dangling, saving her breath to cling to life. The zeppelin we were so safely riding in has exploded in a gaseous hellfire cloud, and it's rapidly descending. Poor Jane was enjoying the view on the balcony's edge when the airship lunged forward, throwing her out of the gondola and along the canopy wall. It's a miracle she's not dead.

She works her leg around the rope like a big-top circus performer, but it's not enough. Even if she hangs on, it won't stop the blimp's collision with the ground, or the stadium walls. The only thing left for me to do is join her. I climb over the balcony and grab hold of the guide rope. It's not made for this kind of pressure, but the fire's too hot to worry about weight limits and physics ratios. Gravity pulls me down, the rope burns my flesh. But I don't let go. I yell down to Jane that I'm here, everything will be okay. Together we swing urgently back and forth as the burning blimp continues its dive. But the motion creates enough arc for us to jump into a glade of lush trees.

We tumble through the branches, our bodies collecting bruises and scratches. Snapping twigs that could be bones crack and give way. Suddenly, our movement stops. We're back on earth. It takes a moment for us to realize we've survived. I hold Jane's hand and we look up through the hole in the trees. She trembles; she is speechless, soundless, only breathing. The smell of burning gas is everywhere, like we've been bathed in it. To our right, plumes of smoke belch and billow, blocking the sun, making the day seem like night. We're safe now, covered only in huge bunches of the giant maple leaves that cushioned our fall from the fiery sky.

"Everything is going to be all right," I tell her, and she believes me.

I sit straight up in bed, shocked into reality, awakened from another crazy dream.

My brain slowly identifies the material objects around me: bed, lamp, clock. I'm in my
room. I'm with a girl. We must've fallen asleep. I look down at
Candyce-not-Jane. She faces me, eyes closed. Her head tilts as
she talks to the dream-people in her dream-office. "She didn't
tell me the meeting was canceled," she says.

Oh God, she sleep-talks?

I get out of bed and amble to the kitchen. Zero's awake too,
thumping his tail against the linoleum. The closer I get, the
quicker he thumps. He prances to the fridge.

"What are you so excited about?"

He stares up at me with anxious eyes, his tail whipping through
the air.

I scratch his head, open the fridge, and dig out some lunch
meat, which starts Zero salivating. Just the sound of the deli bag
wrapper gets him drooling. "Easy," I tell him. "This stuff is terrible for your heart."

He sits, then stands on all fours, then sits again.

I throw him a slice of bologna, which he inhales. At least he's more relaxed. I decide I'm not hungry, but pour a glass of milk. Zero licks his chops, stealing glances toward my bedroom.

"I'm not sure about that girl either, buddy. She talks a lot, but I think she's mostly harmless." I take a strong whiff of the milk, and gag a little. I pour it down the sink drain and run some water. "Don't worry, she probably won't be around much longer."

Zero trots back to his dog bed.

I pour out the rest of the bad milk and get back in bed too. It takes me a while to fall asleep because I'm anticipating more of Candyce's sleep-talking. I stare down at her blue-streaked hair, and it somehow makes me sad. I feel like I want her to be gone, like she's taking up my space, talking at shadows and making it uncomfortable for me to be in my own room. We haven't even done anything serious, but already I want her out. I manage to fall asleep but wake up a while later, with Candyce six inches from my face.

"What time is it?" I ask.

"I was waiting for you to wake up. I was trying to be quiet."

"How long have I been sleeping?"

"All night," she says.

I rub my eyes and sit up and she sits back, legs akimbo.

"I need to tell you something but I don't want you to be mad at me," she says.

"Okay."

She shifts her position on the bed and shakes a last cigarette from the box. She lights it and sucks in the smoke, sizing me up for my potential reaction, then purses her lips and exhales through her nose. She starts to form words but they stop. She tries again, but they're stuck. A vein rises on her neck, pulsating wildly, as if her explanation might be caught behind it.

"What?" I ask.

"Promise you won't be mad."

"How can I promise that? I don't even know what you're talking about yet."

"Just don't get mad."

"Fine," I say, and cross my arms.

"You're getting mad."

"Just say it."

"Okay, okay," she says. "It's just that it's a little weird. I mean, it's not weird for me, but you might think it's weird or you might think I'm weird because of it."

"What is it?"

"I just don't want you to think I'm weird," she says. "Or that I'm lying. It's something that happened last night and I thought I should tell you about it."

I uncross my arms and take her cigarette away to steal a drag. I sit back. I am waiting. Waiting to hear what will make me mad and think she's weird. Then out it comes.

"I think I met your mom last night," she says.

I say nothing. I think my eyebrows go up.

"Not in the normal way, like giving her a hug or shaking hands, she just talked to me, inside my head."

I must be moving away because she creeps a little closer, hopping little hops to close the gap. She whispers, but it's louder than when she talks in her normal voice.

"Every so often I'll hear people talking to me who aren't there," she says. "Not always, only a few times. My grandmother talked to me a year after she died. She just said hello, but your mom was really chatty."

I haven't mentioned anything about Mom to Candyce, least of all the bottle of Bordeaux downstairs, or the times I've had similar experiences. I wonder if Mom is on a rampage, destined to be remembered by talking to everyone who enters my home. I wonder if she can hear me right now, as I discuss her little conversation with Candyce. I wonder why I'm suddenly feeling angry.

"What did she say?" I ask tersely.

"You said you wouldn't get mad."

"I just want to know what my mother said to you."

"She wants to know how you are, mostly. So I told her what you do for a living, and how you met me, and that you came in for a CAT scan but Dr. Singh thinks you're fine, and—"

"You told her all this."

"She misses you. She—"

"Where was I during all this? Why didn't you wake me up?"

"You were sleeping so nicely and I was restless so I got up and went in the kitchen and then I started hearing her voice sort of in my head but not."

"Fascinating."

"You don't believe me."

"It's just very . . ."

"Weird. You think I'm weird and lying."

I am silent.

A smile creeps across Candyce's face; she can't stop it. "She said she likes me."

"Really," is all I can get out.

"She said I was fun. She was excited, asking so many questions."

"Like what? What was she asking that was so exciting?"

"She wants to know where the train to Timbuktu is because she's late for an appointment with the emperor of Japan."

We stare at each other a moment.

"Of course she is," I say.

Candyce's face drops. "I shouldn't have said anything."

"No," I say. "It's okay." But my voice is rising and I can't control it. "I'm just curious what questions my dead mother is asking a girl I've known for less than a month, a girl who I've never even truly fucked and who decided to peruse my home in the middle of the night while having lengthy conversations with my dead mother?"

Candyce sits patiently, her eyes sad. "I see," she says and climbs off the bed. She gathers up her clothes, and quickly gets dressed. "I thought I could trust you; you seemed like a nice guy."

"Did I mention that she's dead?"

She grabs the doorknob to leave, but turns back first. "And you won't ever be fucking me, Sid. Good-bye." Then she walks out and slams the door behind her.

I sit and smoke the rest of her cigarette. I don't even like smoking. It stinks and tastes horrible and last I heard it causes 312 kinds of cancer, as well as heart disease and impotence.

"Timbuktu isn't even in Japan," I say out loud, but I think she's already gone.

Since it's the weekend, I sleep until noon.
I throw some clothes on and go outside to
sit on my front porch. I stare at the mailbox.
Mary Jo is nowhere to be seen, probably because
it's Sunday and that means no deliveries to monitor.

Then I notice someone walking up the street.

A tall man with dark hair and a smooth gait. He's about three
houses away, crossing to my side. He's got a beer in his hand, and
a cigarette dangles from his mouth. His shirt is untucked and he's
barefoot. Something about his posture strikes a chord of recogni-
tion, maybe it's the angle of his shoulders, or how he holds them
back. With each new step, I'm sure I know this man, but until he
is close enough for me to see the gray in his eyes, I don't realize
it's Gerald the Post Office Guy, in civilian clothes.

He continues in my direction, pulls a hit from his smoke, and
follows it up with a swig of beer. A hint of danger energizes the air
as he approaches—an odd sense of unease, the kind that might
accompany witnessing your parents having sex, or seeing Santa
Claus unmasked. I'm so used to seeing Gerald in his uniform,
performing his federal duties, I've never considered he might
have another life outside the United States Post Office.

"I know what you're doing," he says when he gets within speaking distance. He continues to walk closer. "I know all about it." He starts up the porch steps.

"You work at the post office," I say.

He nods and his eyebrows rise. He points at me with his cigarette. "You're good."

I feel duped—an outstanding citizen, a hero of mine, is smoking in my peaceful front yard, pointing at me, drunk. Well, maybe not drunk, but well liquored. At least he's drinking something respectable, although Guinness in a can always struck me as an oxymoron.

Now directly in front of me, he offers his hand. "Most people call me Gerald," he says.

"Sid," I say, and offer my left hand, the nondamaged one, and we shake.

"Nice to officially meet you, neighbor Sid."

I hold up my right hand. "Cut it on a broken glass," I explain, but he couldn't care less what I did to it.

My cell phone rings. I hold my finger up to Gerald. He shrugs. I answer; it's the robot lady. She sounds so pleasant most of the time. But today it's different. She sounds like popcorn—kernels of vowels and shells of consonants popping off the sides of their yellow plastic prison wall.

"This . . . un . . . sage . . . cell . . . one . . . pruv . . ."

I try my best to decipher the words.

"An . . . portant . . . ular . . . serv . . . der . . ."

Apparently it's an important message from my cellular phone service provider. I'm getting cut off due to late payments. I haven't actually had service provided, and now I'm getting cut off. I'm so angry I want to call back and complain, but I know I won't get decent reception where I'm standing. I focus on my new friend.

"I didn't realize you were my neighbor," I say.

"Yep, live a couple streets away." He holds out his cigarette pack: a neighborly offering.

"No thanks. Don't smoke."

He takes another hit. "I enjoy cigarettes," he says, and blows twin columns of smoke through his nostrils like a cartoon bull. "They give me pleasure."

"They also give you cancer."

Gerald doesn't seem to mind. He takes a sip of his Guinness. "Three hundred and twelve kinds of cancer actually, not to mention certain other maladies."

"CNNhealth.com?" I ask.

"Is that where I got that from?"

"Must be. I read the same article."

"I read everything," he says, and points at his cigarette. "I like to know what I'm getting into."

"Heart disease, emphysema, and impotence, according to the latest study."

Gerald waves away my impressive statistics. "That's the least of the world's worries." He takes a final sip, crushes his can. "Crazy, how times change," he says and wistfully searches the sky. "When I was a teenager, I used to take Suzy Schroeder out to the drive-in movies in my Ford pickup truck. We might sneak a couple of the old man's beers. That was the height of our summertime rebellion. Nowadays, kids race around in their modified street cars, texting each other for sex hookups and crystal meth, packing heat and ready to use it. World's headed in a strange direction."

My phone chirps a two-note melody to alert me of the text-message version of the important message I just heard.

Gerald opens his fist to cradle the chunk of crumpled aluminum that was his Guinness. "Do you have any idea how many objects are flying around up there so you can talk on that thing?"

"Not enough, apparently," I say and turn off my phone; it sings a melancholy tune.

Gerald holds the can up like it's a satellite floating across the heavens. "Twenty-five thousand. Twenty-five thousand! And that was last year's count. Probably another five thousand this year alone. It's getting crowded up there. The government ran out of earth to pollute, so now they're polluting space." He coughs. A pale cloud of smoke appears in front of him, freshly discharged from his lungs. "You know, a broken satellite is about to come down and nobody knows where?"

"Really," I say, and instinctively look up.

"Satellite Sixty, they named it. Makes it sound controllable, I guess. Just another number, nothing harmful. But Satellite Sixty is going to crash down on someone's head one day soon. Check that out on your CNN." Gerald drops the can; it lands with a clunk. "So," he says, "enough of the philosophizing. Let's get to it. What are you digging in your backyard?"

"Oh, it's nothing."

"Really?"

"Yeah, it's really nothing."

"Because I've got digging equipment, I could help you out if you need it. Neighbor to neighbor."

"Oh, that's nice, but I'm fine."

"So what is it?" he asks.

"It's a spa."

He nods. "Uh-huh," he says, like he doesn't believe me. He picks up his satellite can and starts to walk toward the backyard without asking. "Well let's take a look."

"Wait—" I yell after him, but he's on a mission. I catch up with him in the back, where he stands at the hole's edge. I feel a little ashamed at the asymmetry of my design. It looks so hacked up, totally unprofessional.

"Some spa," he says with a grin.

I shrug. I can't help it if I don't know what I'm doing.

Gerald considers the dimensions of the hole and steps back, like he's trying to figure what the hell kind of spa would fit in this garbage pit. Then he gets close to me, close enough so I can smell the beer on him.

"You gotta do it in levels and make it square," he says.

We stare at one another for a moment, and then he shakes his head and smiles, like we're sharing a secret, like we're on the same frequency.

"If it's not the taps on your phone, it's the junk in the sky. Gotta hide somewhere. I've got dozens of plans for shelters like this. I'll set you up, no problem."

"Oh, but, it's—"

"Hell, you can have them. I'm already dug in." He nods at the ground, studies the layout of my backyard in relation to my house.

I can't break his enthusiasm. I don't want to provoke him either. "So you have a shelter already?"

A friendly smile grows across his face. "I just like to get away. Somewhere quiet. You know, dark."

I know exactly.

I think Gerald and I are going to be good friends.

Maybe it's our mutual appreciation of peace and quiet, or Gerald's selfless offer to help me with my own dig, but whatever it is, he got me to come underground, and I can already feel the damp air creep into my lungs like a cold ghost.

"Keep going," he implores. I'm first down the makeshift stairs. I reach out to touch the walls for guidance, and as I slowly descend into darkness, I'm beginning to wonder if this was such a good idea. "One step at a time," Gerald coos behind me. The blackness deepens. I hear something metallic clank just over my shoulder, something loose and dangling. With great clarity I realize that this is where I will die: a dark, earthen prison under some psycho mailman's house. Soon I will feel intense blunt pain and for a few horrific moments I will understand with deep, irreversible regret that I have made extremely poor decisions to get myself in this place, slaughtered by a stranger.

A chain pull switch clicks, and a bare bulb fills the room with loud, naked light. Gerald squints dumbly up at it. "I gotta put a forty-watt in there, hundred is way too bright."

My eyes take a moment to recover from the shock, and what I see is the last thing I expect from a Jekyll & Hyde post office worker with a penchant for survivalist practices. Rows and rows of rows of them. They seem to go on forever. I'm so confounded by the sight, I forget to be afraid.

"You know that question, if you were ever stuck on an island with only one book, what would it be?" Gerald asks. I nod along and start counting. Ten aisles of bookshelves each go back at least fifty or sixty feet. All of them, full stacks. It's like a library down here. An underground library. "I could never answer that question," he says. "I love them all."

I roam the aisles. The walls, floor, and ceiling are all covered with wood planks. It feels like the inside of a coffin. I follow a shelf of books with my finger and pull a few titles out. Most of them are library rejects, with plastic jackets and Dewey Decimal System numbers still printed on them. Some of the book's covers are missing. But they're well organized, and there are so damn many of them. I realize I'm tiptoeing, trying to stay quiet in the library. In the back of the room, dehumidifiers hum out a dissonant chord. Massive wood beams in the ceiling would keep a backhoe from falling through.

"Voltaire, Milton, Dickens, Carroll, all the classics," he says. He talks about his collection while I search a different aisle for the real collection—his guns and knives and tear gas. They must be in here somewhere, another trap door, perhaps? "A few plays," he continues. "And in the back is my theology collection. I keep my contemporary books up front."

"Where do you keep your food and water?" I ask from the next aisle over.

I wait for his answer, but there's only silence, and then suddenly he's right next to me, a few inches away. He keeps doing that.

"The only way to survive is to fill yourself with wisdom," he says, and gently taps his temple. "Wisdom is learning from others' experiences. These books are others' experiences. I don't need stockpiles of food." He pulls a book from the shelf and hands it to me. *"Bon appétit*, my boy. Eat up."

"I'm claustrophobic," I say, and turn toward the door.

He steps in front of me. "Then why do you bury yourself in mud?"

Good question. "It's a spa," I explain.

"Right," he says, then gives me a look like he thinks I'm full of shit. "Well, you let me know if you need any help with anything, okay neighbor?" He steps aside.

I give him the thumbs-up and climb the stairs.

"Anything at all!" he calls up after me.

Back at the surface, I look over the span of his yard. His secret library is clearly overextending the boundaries of his neighbors on the west and north of him, and I wonder how far he's planning on going. He seems genuinely interested in helping me, and I feel a little guilty for leaving so abruptly. I start to walk away.

"I'll be down here," Gerald's voice calls from down below, "getting my fill!"

I drag myself through Monday's standard promotion at Wanderlust, and I
drag myself home. My mailbox disappoints
me once again. A few coupons and a magazine
subscription offer, but only one envelope, and it looks disap-
pointingly familiar. Bright red letters read: IMPORTANT ACCOUNT
INFORMATION. OPEN IMMEDIATELY. I open the envelope and more
red letters say: "Your phone will be disconnected in seven days
unless you pay your balance due. If we do not receive payment
within thirty days, you will be reported to a collection agency.
Your credit may be compromised."

I fold the coupon ads around the credit-threat letter and
something slips out and lands on my foot. It's a postcard: sun-
faded and wrinkled, as if it had been dropped in the ocean and
dried in the sun. The front graphic is divided into six squares.
Red letters in the first square say: "Costa Rican Paradise." The
other squares are photos.

Palm Trees.

Crimson-beaked toucans.

A perfect ocean wave, frozen in its inertia.

Waterfalls surrounded by bright green moss.

A couple strolling hand-in-hand on a black-sand beach.

I flip it over. The writing is a mass of blurry, inky symbols and shapes baked into an alien language. There are only two clear words at the very bottom. MORE SOON! it says, and it feels like a promise.

So, another postcard. Illegible for the most part, leaving me to wonder what might be coming soon, but definitely back in the loop. How did it get here? What goes on in these post offices? I can't get my head around it.

This latest arrival and this past weekend's encounters with Candyce and Gerald have left me feeling a little surly. I'm actually glad to be back at work—back in the grind, back within the boundaries of knowing what to expect. I feel like what pregnant women go through after giving birth: they forget the pain of delivery and remember only the positive aspects. They reach a point where it seems like a great idea to try again.

But for me that point is now quickly vanishing during this, my twenty-fifth call of the day. Now I'm starting to wish there was an epidural for telemarketers because this pushy woman will not listen to my advice about Europe.

"And are you sure you want to go to Paris?" I ask.

"Why wouldn't I?"

"Is that safe?"

"Paris, France?" she asks. "I thought those riots were under control now."

"Well, that depends on what you consider 'under control,' " I say.

"Look, don't tell me it's not safe in Paris. My friends were there last month and they said they could walk the streets at night."

I grab Bug-Out Bob off his desk post and give him a few pumps. His eyes bulge and retreat, his ears explode and implode.

"Have you heard about the satellite that's about to fall from the sky?" I ask her.

"Excuse me?"

"There is reason to believe a faulty satellite may fall somewhere over northern Europe in the next few weeks. You haven't heard?"

"That's ridiculous," she says.

"Suit yourself. You could always go to the Galapagos Islands. Those are great."

"I'm not going to buy a more expensive trip because you heard a satellite is going to fall out of the sky. Paris is fine, and it's safe as ever."

I toss the squeeze toy at my desk top. He bounces once and rolls to a stop against the computer monitor.

"You're right, Paris is safe," I say. I search my cubicle walls for promotional posters of Paris, and peel them off. I toss the Eiffel tower in my garbage, tear The Louvre into tiny pieces. "It's a little boring though, isn't it?"

"Excuse me?" she asks, and coughs. I think she might be drinking.

"For Europe, I mean. You sound like the more adventurous type."

"Oh," she says, barely flattered, a little confused. "Well, how about Portugal?"

"Or Spain?" I offer.

"Spain would be fantastic. What packages do you have to Spain?"

"The only thing is . . ." I peel the Barcelona beach poster off my wall, and send it into the trash with the others.

"What?" she snaps. "What's wrong with Spain?"

"I wasn't impressed," I say.

"Then why did you bring it up?"

"Good question. I'm looking at a map here," I continue, and tap my pencil against the bare spots on my cubicle wall. With half of the work posters gone, a checkerboard of tan fabric remains. My latest postcard holds the most promise, with all its flaws and irregularities. It feels the most real. That's why I brought it to work. I tear down the poster of Piccadilly Circus and tack up the Costa Rican Paradise postcard in its place. The happy couple running on the beach in the bottom right square seem to have it all figured out. They look back at me with inviting eyes, enticing me toward their newfound wisdom and happiness. I think about the message on the back: MORE SOON! "What about Costa Rica?" I ask the customer.

"No thanks."

"I hear it's paradise."

"Have you ever been there?"

The headset pinches at my skull, it feels unusually tight today. I wonder if Steve has adjusted the headsets on us to keep us more alert. He would do something like that, just to mess with us. "No, I've never been. Heard a lot of wonderful things, though."

"Yeah, well, if getting your rental car's tires slashed by petty criminals and being robbed in the jungle is your idea of fun, it's all yours," she says.

"Sounds like someone had a bad experience."

"My son had the bad experience. He said the monkeys wouldn't leave him alone, either. Filthy, filthy animals."

"Monkeys are extremely intelligent."

"Well these were just dirty and rude."

"Maybe your son shouldn't have fed the monkeys."

"Excuse me?"

"You heard me."

She made a noise like she'd been choked and then let go. "I thought you called about vacation packages, young man. I will not be lectured on parenting. Not to mention all this business with satellites. Why don't you just tell me where to go for vacation?"

I bite my lip, but it comes out anyway: "Hell is really nice this time of year."

She promptly hangs up and The Randomizer goes to work, erasing any history of our conversation. Steve doesn't click in, so he must have missed it. I got lucky. But then Steve hasn't really been hounding me as much lately, so I think he's given up hope.

I just don't know if I can do this any longer, sell these damn things. Even Bug-Out Bob looks tired, lying on his side, staring into oblivion. I pull out my commission report for the past two weeks, and it's far from impressive. Our weekly call-to-sell ratio report is generated by The Randomizer's computer program, and while they only expect a 1:50 sell rate, my 1:225 is not going to cut it. I need to change something soon, or my friends at the collection agency will be calling me more regularly. And as much fun as it is to dodge them, I've got to keep in mind another gem of advice my dad shared before moving on to the next world: "If you keep doing what you're doing, you'll keep getting what you're getting."

I meditate on his advice and study the postcard from Costa Rica. I look at the squiggly lines that make up the cancellation mark. Who would've stamped this and how would it get lost for so long? Who works at these places? And how can I leave this awful job? I start to corral my thoughts on yellow sticky notes, but before I can tear another one off the pad, the answers to my questions come to me all at once.

chapter

52

The first three hit right on target. Three small stones, launched directly at Gerald's door. A nice grouping, I must say. And since I'm standing a good forty feet from his house, I have to say a damn nice grouping. I throw one more, and I think it hits the doorbell because a trail of lights turn on from the right side of his house to the left—one by one, window squares full of light, all the way to the front door—but that final window stays dark. I'm still not sure about the firearms, that Gerald doesn't have a Saturday night special pointed at me right now, so I yell out: "Hey! It's me. Sid. Your neighbor!"

In response, one by one, left to right, the lights go dark again. When they're all out, a few more moments go by, and finally a dark shape exits the front door.

"What the hell are you doing?" the shadow whispers.

"I need to ask you about something," I whisper back.

"What are you throwing at my house?"

"Pebbles," I say, thinking that *rocks* might sound too reckless.

Gerald steps into the moonlight. He's wrapped in a robe, and has a sleeping mask resting on his head. More whispering. "Why didn't you just push the doorbell?" His right index finger points at his left, then he points his left finger at the doorbell and holds his hands out to me, imploring an answer.

"I didn't want you to shoot me."

Gerald's head goes to the sky, his arms fly out to his sides. "I don't own a gun, Sid," he says in a full, clear voice.

"Sorry. I didn't mean, well, I don't know." I'm still whispering.

"I might strangle you though," he says, and pulls his robe tighter around his waist. "Come on." He motions me inside with a crisp, militant wave.

I follow Gerald through his front door and am struck by yet another surprise when he turns on a light. His home is decorated in Holly Hobby Nightmare—country contemporary gone awry. Rocking chairs and teddy bears. Embroidered pillows and big wood furniture. Fake flowers. Knickknacks. Potpourri burners.

"Do you want some tea?" he asks.

"Your house sure is nicely decorated," I say.

"My wife sells country crafts."

"It's very . . . crafty."

"I'll let her know you like it."

"Wait, you have a wife?" I ask. Another surprise. They keep coming.

He nods. "Charlotte."

"You have a wife named Charlotte?"

"No tea?"

"Sure. Sure, tea would be great. Thanks."

Gerald flips an electric switch on a faux wood-burning stove and fills a copper kettle full of water. He offers me one of two rocking chairs, and we sit, and rock. I wait for Laura Ingalls Wilder to walk down the hallway, rubbing her eyes, asking for Pa.

"So what's with the midnight awakening? You scared the crap out of me."

Psychos don't scare so easy, I want to say, but just then a little girl walks down the hall. She doesn't rub her eyes, just widens them as far as they will go. She clutches a teddy bear to her chest.

"It's okay, Pumpkin," Gerald says. "Go back to bed." The child turns right around and does as she's told. No blinking, no questions. I decide right then that Gerald is not a psycho, he's just misunderstood. By me, primarily. Maybe he really is a normal guy who sorts mail all day in order to provide for his Amish wife and zombie spawn. "You want to browse the library, don't you?" he asks.

"Oh, yes," I lie, "but that's not why I'm here."

"It really is something, isn't it? You know, it's not locked. Next time go ahead and peruse the aisles. It would be better than waking up the family."

"Thanks. That means a lot."

We both rock some more. He, slow and easy. Me, quick little spurts. A quiet stream of vapor emits from the copper kettle. Gerald gets up and fetches us two cups and teabags. He pours each of us a full cup of hot water, sits back down, and continues his slow rock.

"So, what, you want to use my digging equipment? It's a little late to run that stuff, neighbor."

"No. No, that's not it." We both stop rocking and sit in silence for a while, awkward, waiting for the tea to brew. A Raggedy Ann doll in a baby wicker chair stares ominously at me. I'm not sure how to ask, so I just let it out. "I need a job, Gerald."

"You don't have a job?"

"No, I have a job. It just doesn't pay very well. I need some extra hours. I thought your guys hired for temporary help occasionally."

"Sure, but it's crazy work. Drives you nuts."

"I really think I can handle it."

"I'd hate to subject you to it."

"It can't be that bad."

Gerald grimaces, looks down the hall, then back at me, down at my hand.

"How are you going to work with that?"

"It's practically healed," I say, which isn't a total lie. The cut stopped throbbing a while ago, and I'm already using it more than I should. "I wish you'd consider it," I say.

He nods at me. Simulated embers float up in the stove's belly. I think they're bits of tin foil. "Be careful what you wish for," he says.

"How about just for a month? Really, I want to try this. I need the extra money."

Gerald swirls his tea around and stares at the bottom of his cup. "It's good to want things," he says, then downs the tea and stares at me again, the orange glow of the stove casting long shadows across his face.

"You're still mad about the pebbles, aren't you?" I ask.

I'm not sure, but I think a grin creeps over his face.

The monotony of everything about this place is driving me crazy. Gerald was right. The damn mail keeps coming and coming and coming and no way will it ever stop. Stacks of it, hordes and hordes of it. Endless.

Being a temp guy, I have a different-colored shirt. I'm the one in red instead of gray, which makes me think they've dressed me up in a warning. Watch out for the red guy, he's new. He might not be able to take it.

. I do the math in my head: how many people inhabit the earth, how many letters they might send on a daily average, how many of those people live in my city, and how many of their letters might come down my conveyor belt. It's too many. It's never-ending. The people will keep writing letters and paying bills and then sending them and the envelopes will keep coming, and there will never be a break on my conveyor or any other for that matter. I am completely hopeless against such a force. I've only been here for two hours.

I can't take it. I need a break. I need to stop looking at zip codes and addresses. I need to stop hearing that droning, pulsating, trance-inducing hum, need to let my eyes rest from the flurry of corners and edges and stamps and plastic windows.

My neck itches. The mail keeps coming. I arch my sore back for relief. And the mail keeps coming. I stomp my feet a few times to get them to wake up. I scratch my neck. The rollers roll. The envelopes whiz by. Finally, I make a dam with one arm across the conveyor, and the mail floods over the top, like logs in a river.

"Sid," Gerald says from somewhere.

"What?" I pull my arm off the line.

"Come here," he says. He's standing right behind me, dressed in his uniform, clean and serious like I remember him. It helps me relax a little. He waves me toward him, a few feet away from my station. I stand up and leave the mail to its own devices. We face each other. His gray eyes are calm, his demeanor still that cool professional level I admire, especially today. But as he studies me, I consider that maybe he's left his soul at home, and that's how he manages so well here. He sips his coffee. "Sid, why don't you take a coffee break?" He nods up to a small room on the second level, and immediately I feel better; it looks soundproof.

I follow the yellow tape on the floor as Gerald instructed, and upon my arrival, plunk a few coins in the coffee machine. It winds up and makes a few knocking sounds, which is nice because I know it's working. It's trying, at least. A cardboard cup drops onto the slotted platform and the coffee begins to brew. The silence and the smell are exactly what I need.

At first it was fun, working in the sort room. The spectacle of all those conveyors and slots and bags and rollers was really quite something, how the packages move from place to place, how they're sorted and carried from here to a complicated system of hubs and drop points, trucks and planes, jeeps and snowmobiles.

I realized early on though—probably in my first twenty minutes—that I'm not cut out for postal sorting.

"I'm sorry, I should leave," I tell Gerald as soon as he steps inside the safety of the coffee room. I can't hear the belts churning downstairs, but I can see the repetitive movements of the machines, and it's enough for my imagination to fill in the blanks. *Nyhuh nyhuh*, go the machines, *nyhuh nyhuh nyhuh*.

"Forget about your little episode downstairs. Everybody goes through that. Really. I want you to stay." He chucks me on the shoulder.

"It's good to want things," I say, and stare at my coffee.

After my break, Gerald sends me over to the truck-loading wing. He says there's much need for help over there. So I help. I build walls by forming *T*'s with packages. A stream of boxes slide down a long chute into the semitrailer: long, brown packages that weigh nothing and tiny gift boxes filled with lead. What is in all these boxes? Where are they all going? More and more boxes arrive, like a maddening game of life-size Tetris, only with no cool theme music, and no escape. I'm sure by now that this probably won't make me enough money to pay for my bills *and* cover the psych meds I'll need to survive here.

One motivated jock has a bright attitude, though. He's a meaty guy, someone who does a lot of pushups. I never catch his name, but whenever we're both at the end of our respective trailers, he waves to me and says, "It's just like getting paid to work out, huh?" and then he rolls down the trailer door, bangs it twice, and waves at the truck as it pulls away—a job well done.

It's just like getting paid to be mentally tortured, I want to say, but I keep my mouth shut and smile at him just enough so he can't tell if I'm smiling or not. Gerald has warned me in his own way to stay cool, and I'm determined to make good after my late-night visit. Somehow I finish my day and tell Gerald thanks and make my way back home.

The drive home feels surreal, as if I floated all the way. I make it inside and stretch out on the floor with Zero. I stare at the blank white ceiling for a while, but every time I blink I see packages. If I close my eyes, the boxes descend upon me and then I'm trapped, stuck behind my own eyes. Eventually I get so tired I fall asleep without realizing it, only to have a nightmare about mail being shoved under my door. It's Mary Jo from across the street doing the shoving, and she's cackling hysterically. "You've got mail!" she screams. "You'd better do something!"

When the soil slides between your toes,
when you feel the earth seeping into your
ears, blocking out the sounds of the living
world, when it's covering your eyes so all the light
is shut out and you're totally surrounded by serene darkness—
that's when you know you're fully committed to the mud bath.

Some folks fear commitment because they fear their loss of
freedom. But when you totally commit yourself to something, you
free yourself from the burden of wasting your energy on other,
less worthy things. Right now I'm completely unencumbered by
forty-five pounds of backyard soil. It may not be mineral-rich
like the spa's Moor peat mud, but it seems to be doing the trick.

"What the fuck are you doing?" a muffled voice asks from the
top of the hole. Her acrid tone is easy to recognize, even through
my plugged ears. It's Candyce. "Why is there a hole in your backyard? And why are you in it?"

I drag my hands out of the thick mud, and a loud sucking
sound tells me I finally got the consistency right. I scrape the mud
off my eyes and open them. They must look like two eggs in the
bottom of a giant frying pan, from her perspective. This makes
me smile. She stands with her arms crossed, one hip cocked hard

to the right. If I do look like two eggs at the bottom of a pan, she doesn't find it amusing.

"Hello? Can you even hear me?"

"Mm-hmm," I say, the humming quite loud in *my* ears.

She huffs, appalled, I think, that I'm not explaining myself, that I'm not jumping up to meet her. She tosses a piece of paper down at me as hard as she can. It floats down, against her intentions, and gently lands near my right hand. "Dr. Singh's results on your CAT scan. I thought you'd want to see them."

I delicately pinch the paper between muddy thumb and index finger, pinky extended as if I'm about to sip tea. Candyce shakes her head and stomps away from the hole's edge. A series of scratches and dots make up Dr. Singh's handwriting, and next to that, more studied, deeply slanted letters. The legible handwriting says: "Normal." Candyce's translation. My CAT scan is normal.

I sit up to celebrate. The mud slides down my chest and back, cold and heavy. My nose is at ground level. I look across the yard, and there is Candyce, walking back to her car. "I'm normal," I say. She gets in her car and slams the door. "I'm normal!" I say again, louder this time, but she can't hear me. I carefully stand up and step out of the hole, back on solid ground, waving madly at her, my body black and melting, my hair matted and wet. "I'm normal!" I yell at her, "I'm normal!" But she drives away.

Across the street, Mary Jo stands by her mailbox. I wave the paper at her, my egg-eyes wide. "Look," I say, and smile broadly at her, but my elation is misconstrued as something sinister.

"I don't swim!" she yells, and runs back in her house.

I am in a celebratory mood. My clean CAT-scan results have had a galvanizing effect on my life outlook. I need to get away from this house, out among people and activity, even if they're strangers, maybe especially so. I take a long, cleansing shower, get dressed, and head over to The Basement on Longley Street.

The Basement has jazz playing 24-7 and unwritten menus— you order what you want and they improvise. Most important, people come here to relax, read, and get juiced up on caffeine. I order a double espresso, and find the darkest corner available. I've decided to bring the postcards. I plan on meticulously studying them until I find the one elusive detail that explains everything. A lot can be learned from the details. I stack them in a neat pile and begin.

It's only after holding the third one up to the light that I realize Jane from yoga class is here too, and she's stealing glances in my direction. I can't tell if she recognizes me right off, or if she just thinks it's odd that I'm reading a stack of postcards, but here we are, two semi-strangers, aware of each other's presence.

Jane is plain. That's why I like her. That's what makes her

beautiful. I don't really know much about her, not even her real name. I like to think she spends a good amount of her time sipping warm coffee drinks here, alone, and meditating on mountain tops. Well, hill tops.

Jane has a few contradictions about her, like how she sits near the front window but then covers her face from the sun. She could easily move away. I imagine she sits in the window because she likes to drink her coffee while she drinks in the life of the city street. A quiet, curious type. Habitual in her habits, reclusive, yet seeks the company of others, though not necessarily directly. She would be a mountain gorilla in the Great Apes documentary I watched last week: fiercely intelligent, mostly solitary, but could die of loneliness if she doesn't have the occasional company of a mate. That's Jane, sipping on her latte, thinking deep thoughts, vaguely dissatisfied, searching for something deeper, something real. But for all I really know, she could be a rabid baboon, subject to impulsively flashing her sex flower for all the other baboons to see. It's a vulgar thought. I opt for mountain gorilla: pensive, reflective, mysterious.

I wonder if she somehow psychically shared my crashing zeppelin dream, and now she's looking over to me to give thanks for my rescuing her, to celebrate our survival together. I wonder if she's had any similar nocturnal visions about me. Of course, I'll never ask her. Suddenly I'm tired. I don't have the energy to go introduce myself. Something is drawing me to do so, but even if I did, what would I say? "Hello, mysterious gorilla. I know I look tired and disheveled, but I've been working weird hours at a new job and obsessing over the postcards my vanished girlfriend has been sending me. Don't worry, we're not together anymore. Would you like another latte?" It's better if I sit here, quiet. Nothing bad can happen if I just sit in my dark corner and sulk.

"Sid?" a voice pleads from the darkness. "Are you freaking serious?"

I shut my eyes tight in hopes of becoming invisible.

"Well?" the voice implores. It's Candyce. She has spotted me, and there is no mistake on her part. Footsteps clop loudly toward my quiet, gloomy little corner. She's got two hissy-fit friends in tow, both of them dressed in black, with tri-colored streaky hair cut in a shoulder-length bob fashion. "Jesus Christ, Sid. Are you following me now?" she asks. "Is that your new tactic?" She gains strength from her cloned disciples. Their necks bob and weave, their eyes agog, puffs of air pushed through pursed lips. It's like a bad nature show, these three warning the others in the herd about me. "Well?" she asks.

I sip my coffee.

"Is the mud hole not working out anymore?" Her friends snicker and sneak glances at each other.

I add more creamer, watch the little white swirls lighten the entire cup to a paler shade of brown.

"What, are you mute now too?"

Yes, I am. I am mute now.

She hisses through her teeth. Something caustic builds inside her, the final alarm that will let everyone in hearing distance know to stay clear of me, the dangerous predator.

It comes like this: *"Freak."*

It's a whisper, but said with such clarity and conviction that it's more effective than a screech monkey's scream. She has caught the attention of everyone. I am a freak. A stalker freak, with something about a mud hole left undefined, which leaves room for dangerous thoughts in the public's imagination.

The triple threat walks defiantly away. I close my eyes again, this time to reverse a slowly rising headache. Flashes of light relent beneath my lids in a quiet, staccato surge. When I open them, Candyce and her girls have rounded the corner into the main room. I look over to see if Jane witnessed this scene, but she is gone too. This makes me sad, like I've lost something else. Something important.

It's to my great relief when I leave The Basement that Jane is outside on the sidewalk. I start to walk in the opposite direction so she won't think I'm a stalker freak, and she coughs. I turn back, and she's looking at me.

"Did you say something?" I ask.

She shakes her head.

"Sorry," I say and turn away.

"You like to travel, huh?" she asks.

"I'm looking for someone," I mumble, then turn around to look at her.

"I didn't hear you."

"Yes, I like to travel," I say.

"Me too."

We both nod at the sidewalk.

"You've been around?" she asks, motioning toward my postcards.

I have them clutched in my right hand like a child holds a balloon. I stuff them in my back pocket. "A few places. Different countries."

"I've been to Dublin," she says.

"Really? How did you like it?"

"It was rainy. But I loved it. Great people."

More nodding.

"I've been to Barcelona," I offer, but can't think of anything to add.

"How was that?"

I look up at the sky to search for an answer. A jet plane flies just outside the proximity of its sound. "It was bright," I say.

"I bet."

"Look, those girls back there—"

She waves them off. "I know."

"You know them?"

"I know their type," she says, and wrinkles her nose.

Then she does this amazing thing. She smiles at me, real, simple. I try to smile back but I'm afraid it's more like a wince.

We both study the ground again. Words come out of me that I don't expect, and then she says words too, and then she writes something and hands me a piece of paper and I do the same, and she waves and walks away.

I look down at what she wrote: Melanie. My Jane is named Melanie.

And somehow we've exchanged phone numbers and I'm left standing on the sidewalk wondering what got me to this new place that only moments before was abject humiliation. I hold her number tightly between my finger and thumb like it's a winning lottery ticket. But nobody knows I've won, and even I don't know how much is in the jackpot, which makes me happy and nervous and thrilled and sad all at once.

I know there will be bruises on my waist
the next day, she's hanging on that tight. I
don't blame her. Speeding across cold water
on a Jet Ski at fifty mph can be a little scary.

It's a vivid, cold, amazing dream. "Lean into me!" I yell back
at Melanie. We both cower down into the wind, creating one sleek
aerodynamic unit, protecting ourselves from the icy sea spray as
we bash through the waves. A sheet of water splashes over us. I
keep my hand on the throttle. Another wave slides across our
backs. Her grip around me is unyielding.

The night hides us as we speed up the coast, away from the bad
people who follow. We can't see them, but they're close, bearing
down on us, just outside our periphery. The continuous jarring
against the waves is taking its toll. I wonder if we'll make it.

Melanie says something into my back, a worried murmur. I
feel it more than hear it. She can't take the running anymore.
She's losing feeling, it's too cold. Her grip loosens a bit, a weak-
ening in her attachment to me, to this vehicle. All around us is
the vast, surging ocean.

I back off the throttle. Only one thing to do. I turn the Jet Ski
around and head straight back into the source of our turmoil.

My heroine is startled but I can feel an uptick in her excitement. She too knows it's the only way, and I've done the only thing that can be done. Melanie's grip finds new strength, and I pull down on the gas once again. This time, I don't even feel the cold of the water because we're flying now, floating over the chop of the black waves, a storm cloud on its way to deliver a punishing release.

The Randomizer picks a number and I wait for someone to answer. I'm decked out in my plastic headset and hands-free microphone, staring through the cubicle wall ahead of me as I try to construct a face from some stranger's floating voice. This someone will almost certainly be in their home, and I will be transported to their living room through their earpiece and into their ear, inside their head, my alien voice taking up space in their mind for a few choice moments. What an incredible opportunity. But all I've got to talk about is cruise ships and five-star hotels.

I daydream about a mile-long, touch-less car wash, the kind that pulls your car along after you throw it in neutral. This automatic wonder has four cycles of soap and a quarter-mile drying track that leaves your car spotless. It's twenty minutes of high-tech dirt eradication, a marvel of modern times. Space-age suds.

A distant voice in my ear wants to know who I am.

I steady my mic between forefinger and thumb. This is ground control, I say, and we've got another one ready to go on the Miracle Mile. Throw it into neutral and off you go. Imagine the serenity. Experience the bliss. This is no ordinary clean.

"I'd buy some if I knew what it was," the voice says.

The Randomizer has made a connection. I know from the sound of her voice that she is five-foot-four, a waitress at the local mall. She smokes. She doesn't condition her hair enough and doesn't read much, but when she does it's romance novels, and she's not embarrassed to say so.

"Sorry ma'am, just trying to set the stage," I say. "This is Sid from Wanderlust, and I have an exciting offer to tell you about."

"Go on, Sid." She sucks on a cigarette—a wet, dirty sound. "Tell me all about it. Tell me every naughty little detail."

"When's the last time you took a vacation?" I ask.

"What's the big deal?" Natalie asks. "It's a phone call. You make them all day long."

I want to tell her that it's not a big deal to her because she's not the one making the phone call. This is not some memorized pitch. There's nobody inside my ear coaching me on this one. I pace across the kitchen floor, my cell in the crook of my neck, and check the fridge again, as if there will be something new inside, on this, my third opening of the door. I'm also wondering why my cell phone connection only achieves crystal clarity when I'd rather not be talking on it.

"If you don't want to go out with her, that's fine," she says.

"I do. I want to."

"Good. Then call her."

"I can't."

"You can't?"

"I have some things I need to finish."

"Oh," she says, like she's heard that one before.

"Maybe next week."

"She gave you her number, right? Don't keep her hanging or she'll be history."

It doesn't feel like I've been ignoring her. Lately Melanie has been in my head in strange ways. She returns to my thoughts like a satellite in orbit. Her faint signal passes my ears, again and again, barely audible, but constant, reaching from somewhere out in deep space that might not even exist anymore, like a lost ancient wisdom spinning through the sky. I want this wisdom, but I fear losing it. Losing her. Losing something else.

"I do want to call her. Just not this week," I say.

"Not this *week*?"

"Next week would be better."

"What are you doing that's so important you can't call a girl?"

I slide the kitchen curtains open and peer into the backyard— the mud mouth of my homemade spa yawns dreamily up at the night sky. "Big project."

Natalie sucks at her teeth, pushes air back through the gaps, in and out, louder and louder. This is the hideous sound she makes when she feels she's being lied to but doesn't have the energy to argue. "Well, call her when you're not busy," she says, "or let me know and I'll call her. Just don't leave her hanging, okay?"

"I won't."

"Say it."

"What?"

"Promise you won't leave her hanging."

"I promise I won't leave her hanging," I say plainly, but feel panicked.

She sucks at her teeth again. "Well," she says, "I'll let you go. Have a good one."

I hang up the phone and a pressure builds in my chest that feels like oversized shirts stuffed in a tiny closet. I take a deep breath and exhale slow and one of the shirts goes away. I walk out to the garage, and another shirt is gone. I grab a shovel, and with each step through the dewy grass of the backyard I feel lighter, clearer somehow, ready to move earth under the sparkle of the stars.

As I dig, the sweat pours out of me. I'm going through a transformation, but I'm not sure if it's from life to death or death to life. I feel like other zombies might be approaching soon, around the corner at any moment, each of them lying down in their own graves with dreamless sleep and hopeless sighs. I wonder if I will join them.

Today I wouldn't mind if a postcard arrived from Tokyo. I might be tempted to travel to Japan, and I hear there's an entire class of people who live in six-by-three-foot tubes stacked so high they need ladders to reach them. Rows and rows of little tombs, people existing inside plastic cocoons, a city full of morphing insects.

The TV news says a story is coming up that may leave me shocked and dismayed. It's about my drinking water. I sit through two commercial breaks and still no water story. I wonder if there might be something wrong with our copper pipes, but then the news people return to caution me that it's about what might be in my actual water. It's not what I'd expect. One more break and they tell me if I drink enough water, it could have unexpected results.

I go to the kitchen and drink a full glass. And almost exactly as I finish swallowing the last of it, the feeling comes: a woozy, ringing-head sensation. The news was right; it's not what I expected. Suddenly lilacs are in full bloom in my kitchen. The sweet scent fills me up and ruins my vision. My skin begins to tingle, little electric sparks that flow up my arms and down my spine.

And while mentally I feel shocked and dismayed, deep down I'm peaceful. It's a strange juxtaposition.

"I can't be late," a voice says, "they'll leave without me."

It's Mom. Her voice is faint. I instinctively walk toward the basement stairs.

"Mom," I say, "can you hear me?"

"Let me through, I must get on this bus," she says.

"What bus, Mom?" I walk down a few stairs and her voice intensifies.

"I'll be late!"

"What bus?"

"I can't be late," she's yelling now. "It's important!"

"I can hear you. Let me help."

"Oh, you all forgot about me and now I'm late. I can't be late."

"Where are you going?" I ask. Lilacs have followed me. I can practically taste them, bitter petals on my tongue.

"I must make it there."

I go down the rest of the stairs and lean in next to the wine bottle thinking that maybe if I'm closer, she'll hear me better. "Where do you need to be?"

"Don't act like you don't know," she says.

My flesh freezes. Did she really hear me? Was Candyce telling the truth? Somehow this doesn't make me feel better. "What do you mean? How would I know?"

"Everybody knows the bus to Timbuktu should've been here already," she says, although now it sounds like she's talking to someone else entirely—some kind of supernatural ticket clerk? "You can't be late for the Emperor of Japan!"

I don't know what to do. She sounds upset. I try to console her. "You'll make the bus, don't worry," I say. "It just pulled up, time to get on."

Slowly the lilacs fade and the voices with it, as if in direct response to my words. My skin loses its chill and my balance returns, and while the trouble seems to be over, I wonder what it means that I'm all alone in my basement squatting over a bottle of wine.

A pair of female bronze legs walk toward me, their gait swift. They seem to have a conviction about them, a purpose all their own, as if they're disconnected from their body. They are sleek, toned, and strong—not to be messed with. If I weren't lying under forty pounds of cool earth, I might sit up to take a better look at what rests above them. For now, her top half is hidden in the dark shadows caused by the bright sun behind her. I'm back at the spa because I couldn't get the shape of my backyard spa right. The contours were all off, the whole aesthetic blown by inferior corners. So now I lie back in a professional outdoor mud spa, a ceramic tub filled with plenty of the good stuff. My phone, ice water, lemon slice, and complimentary towels rest on a nearby table.

My cell phone rings. I manage to squirm one hand to the surface to check the number. I don't recognize it. Because I seem to be attracting the unknown lately, I'm especially cautious. The two bronze legs have come to an abrupt stop at the edge of my bath. I flip open my phone. "Hello?"

"Is this, uh, is this Sid?" It's a woman's voice: soft, misunderstood, friendly.

"Who's this?"

"Melanie. We met at the coffee shop. If this is Sid."

"Oh. Jane. Hello."

"Jane?" she asks.

"No, this is Sid. Hello? Did you say Melanie? Hi!"

I pull my other arm from the muck to shade my eyes. The sun radiates from behind the owner of the legs. It's Gazelle, and she's holding my credit card up like a question. "Mr. Higgins—"

I nod. She doesn't nod back. "Sorry Melanie, I was talking to someone else. I'm, uh, I'm at a restaurant."

"Oh, maybe I should call another time?"

Gazelle taps her foot, shifts her weight from leg to leg. "We have a problem."

"That might be better," I say. "Is that okay? Maybe I shouldn't have answered. That was rude." I give Gazelle the okay sign. She's not okay.

"I thought maybe we could get coffee sometime," she says.

"Of course, yes. Coffee. I love coffee." Melanie laughs at this. *I love coffee.* Very smooth. I laugh too then, for too long. *Coffee. Ha ha ha.*

I wish I could tell Melanie about how telephone conversations in general make me anxious. I can never express with full intention what it is I'm trying to say. There is so much slippage, so many missed implications and lost nonverbal actions, it's a bit perplexing.

She says something in a funny voice. "Iced coffee is cool," I think she says.

She must be trying to be funny, so I laugh because I think it's polite to respond to her joke. But then I realize I haven't spoken in too many moments and I'm pretty sure it comes across as a stonewall to her attempt at levity, which she's using to cover up her surprise over my rudeness of answering the phone when I'm too busy to talk. The silence grows heavier; I feel it press against me.

"Well," I say, "let's get together, then. Can you call me back in a little while?"

"Sure I can. Enjoy your meal."

"What? Oh, yes, very good. Yum-yum." Does anyone actually *say* yum-yum?

I clap the phone shut. Gazelle, once a coltish beauty, now towers over me like a megalith, arms crossed, her resolute figure refusing to block the noon sun from my photosensitive eyes. She wants me out. I'm not quite sure what to do, so I take a deep breath and sink below the surface.

chapter

61

The boy doctor who recently gave me
stitches now has the pleasure of setting
my pinky. He is bursting with questions but
too embarrassed to ask them. Questions like:
Why are you so dirty? Is this new injury from another fall? Who
was the supermodel who brought you in, and why did she tell the
nurse to make you pay cash?

And I have similar questions, but not nearly as immediate,
although worthwhile nonetheless. Questions like: Who would
guess that the Arizona Day Spa has two security staff ready and
willing to forcibly extract bad-credit customers from their mud
baths? And what were they so angry about? They've never had a
credit card rejected before?

Chip gently separates my pinky finger from my ring finger
and asks if it hurts. Then he touches my elbow and asks if that
hurts. He does this touching and asking for a while, and I alter
my response from a grunt to a head-shake. In between pokes
he looks me over with hangdog eyes. One of his jabs makes me
suck air through my teeth. Satisfied, he skips over to the medical
supply cabinet, and away from my grimy body.

"Digging a swimming pool," I loudly offer. The doctor continues his supply search, rummaging through boxes, opening and closing cabinet doors. "Thought I'd jump in early, fell on the slope of the deep end."

He holds up a roll of white tape like it's found treasure, then grabs a yardstick of metal and foam. He turns to face me. "This will only take a minute."

As if on cue, a young woman down the hall screams for her life. I jump.

The doctor is unfazed. He's put in his time down here in the ER. This makes me feel a little better. The woman screams again. "I want to die," she shouts. "Let me die already." This, followed by the sloppy sounds of vomit spattering on tile.

The doctor begins his work: focused, intense, but moving with ease. "Kids," he tsk-tsks. "Too many of them coming into the ER full of alcohol or drugs, or both." He bends the metal-and-foam bar over my pinky and wraps the tip up with tape. "Wasn't like that when I was a kid," he says.

When was that, last year? I want to ask. But he's doing such a confident job I keep my inside thoughts inside. He seems to have entered manhood in between my injuries. My pinky feels better already.

Then he says, "You're going to feel a little pressure."

I wince because I've never heard that line and experienced good things afterward.

"I haven't done anything yet," he says, and then, quickly, "Okay, here we go." His squeeze adds the promised pressure, while adding nausea to my list of ailments.

"Extra-strength Tylenol should kill the pain," he says. "Let me know how that splint holds up." He clutches my other hand and brushes his thumb over the scar. I flinch. "Looks like that healed really well. You're a fast healer. Your pinky should be good as new in no time."

The moaning down the hall winds up again, quickly escalating to a holler. In scolding tones, a nurse reminds the patient it's her own fault she's eating barium-chalk sandwiches. "I hate you!" the voice shrieks. "I just want to die!"

My cell phone rings. It's my new friend Melanie. I can't answer with all this noise. I pick up my pace going down the tiled hallway, careful not to bump my bionic pinky against anyone. My footsteps echo off the walls. So does the ringing of the phone.

Ring!

Shit. I can't *not* answer.

"I hate you, bitch!" the junkie yells. "Go to hell!"

Ring!

Unhappy faces in the hallway. I remember cell phones aren't allowed in hospitals. Nurses snap their fingers. Doctors shake their heads.

Ring!

"Kill me now!" the junkie screams.

Snap, snap.

Walking faster.

Ring!

"Hey, buddy," someone yells, "turn off your phone!"

I spin around to confront the yeller, to let them know I'm trying, and promptly slam my pinky into the wall. I suck air through my teeth.

Bright stars of pain.

Pressure, my doctor would call it.

The phone falls silent. I scurry down the hall a few more steps, but see Melanie has not left a message. My escape was in vain.

The junkie releases another primal scream. It bounces from wall to wall, off the ceiling and across the hall to meet me with a final exclamation point, as if to transmit the entire hospital's disdain for me.

My pinky throbs in time with my racing heartbeat, a pulsing radio signal sent out to all who might be listening. Enough already, the signal says, I've had enough. The demon junkie laugh-sobs behind me as I step through the automatic doors. Outside, blinding brightness. I squint into the sun. I can already feel a headache coming on.

It was summer when Zoe and I moved in together. Balmy heat. Sticky skin and heavy lungs. Our little love nest was not receiving the cross-breeze we were promised by the landlord. Instead, stale air. I wanted to be as stationary as possible, so I sat at the foot of our futon: slumped shoulders, mouth slack, as if this might make breathing easier. There I sat, waiting for the night to arrive and deliver its cool air.

Zoe was doing something unnecessary in the kitchen. She'd been moving about a lot that day, even in the heat, pacing between the bedroom and the kitchen and the bathroom. Doing nothing tasks. Wiping counters. Rinsing clean dishes. Rearranging items in the fridge. Putting them back as she had found them. Finally, she stopped with the fidgeting.

"Do you remember what your most recent love note said to me?" she called out.

It took a moment for my brain to turn back on. "What?"

"You said you loved doing anything with me."

"I do."

"And then you listed everything we do together."

"Yeah?" By this time, I had slouched into the kitchen. She

stood with her arms crossed, looking out the window, a dishrag hanging from one hand.

She turned to look at me then, an accusatory glare. "Do you know what the list was?"

I looked up at the ceiling, then back at her. I waited for her to tell me.

"Watching TV. Sitting on the couch. Eating dinner."

"Uh-huh."

"Well?" she asked.

"Sorry for enjoying those things with you?"

"We don't *do* anything," she said, and snapped the dishrag in the air. "We sit on the couch. Watch TV."

"Eat dinner," I added.

She took a deep breath and let her cheeks inflate with the exhale.

"You've been thinking about this for a while," I said.

"I need to see more."

"All right."

"I need to see a lot more."

"All right!"

"Sid, I want to travel," she said. "I want to see everything." She twisted the rag in her hands.

"That's a lot."

She shook her head. "I knew you wouldn't get it."

"I'm sorry. What do you want to see? Tell me."

"I want to see the streets of London, the cafés of Paris, the churches of Barcelona, the rain forests of Costa Rica. There's so much out there. I want to get out of here. I don't want to sit on this couch ever again."

"Let's do it."

She looked around the apartment, at the walls, at the floor. "You don't really want that," she said, then looked back at me again.

"Sure I do." Her eyebrows rose a little, almost in a hopeful expression, but then it changed to something else, something I didn't recognize. I tried to get back the hopeful expression. "Let's start in Costa Rica," I offered. "Mountains and oceans, hiking and surfing. It'd be great! I hear the monkeys come right up to you like deer at a petting zoo. I love monkeys."

"I don't mean—I mean, I guess I don't want that. I think I need to do this alone."

"You want to travel the world alone?"

She nodded. I stared at the floor. She was right; I didn't want that. I didn't want her to travel the world alone, and I didn't really see how anyone could want that—to be alone. Maybe there was something I was missing. "Well that's the last Hallmark card I write my own message on, that's for sure."

Her expression remained serious. "I'm sorry. I've always felt like I don't belong here, like where I should really be is a million miles from here. I need to go there."

"That's pretty far."

"Please try to understand," she said.

I thought at the time that her need to explore might be due to my problem with sustaining happiness, although I never found out if she even knew that it was a problem. But there were times when Zoe and I would be having a happy moment, a sweet occasion like a shared laugh, or simply walking down a sidewalk hand in hand after a movie. And maybe we would exchange an inside joke and smile and kiss and blush like teenagers, or stroll along with the confidence of trusting lovers. When experiencing these moments, my imagination would often take over and finish the scene with something dreadful. A van careening around the corner and masked men kidnapping Zoe at knifepoint. A street thug snatching her purse and shooting us dead. A homeless man asking for money, and after we drop a coin in his coffers, he tosses acid in our faces; screaming, we clutch at our melting flesh.

Sometimes when Zoe and I were lying in bed, we'd spoon and drift off to sleep, but my body would twitch and I'd be awake again. I'd sit straight up and look down at her, waiting for her to tell me the news she'd been hiding for weeks but had been afraid to reveal. "What is it," I'd ask. "What is it already?" And then she'd look up at me with teary, red eyes. "I'm dying," she'd say, "I've only got three weeks to live. I don't know how else to say it." And then we'd sit there together, hugging each other, staring at the walls, waiting for them to whisper answers to us, because we wouldn't have any and there would be nothing else to do.

During our trip to Manhattan, Zoe and I had coffee at a sidewalk café. We were enjoying ourselves tremendously, watching the people, feeling the hum of the city, listening to the languages float by. And this guy kept looking over at us, studying something about us, something that was more interesting to him than the other millions of people on the island. And soon my thought became that he was sizing us up. We were clearly tourists, and after we finished our coffees, we were sure to be stabbed in the park. And why? Because the happy moment was lasting all day long. It was an endless happy moment, an inexplicable thing I didn't trust—something so extraordinary and awesome that only a complicated, paranoid evil plot could balance out the universe.

So when Zoe asked me to understand about her wanting to travel alone, I nodded. This would make her happy, and maybe she could sustain it better without me around. She touched my shoulder and let her hand slide down my arm until she was holding my hand, and I agreed to try to understand, and I went about pretending it was okay that she wanted to be a million miles away without me.

From then on, the only distance covered was the space between our conversations. When we did talk, it was usually about a new culture or language, or a city that neither of us had visited. Places nobody in our entire hometown had ever visited. *National Geographic* stuff. Impressive-looking locations. I really did try to understand, but I don't think I ever got there. What I am beginning to understand is that Zoe never got to where she wanted to go, either. She didn't make it a thousand miles, let alone a million. In fact, she stopped about three hundred feet from the Highway 20 overpass. That's what the police report said, anyway. I should ask Zero. He was there.

Melanie and I agree to meet at The Basement; it's our familiar safe ground. The dining section is quiet and intimate, with steel-brushed, round metal tables and chairs with funky fabric patterns. A single purple flower stands in the vase on the table, the only thing between us, besides the table itself.

Melanie looks so alive, I find myself staring at her. I've spent so much time studying her from afar, I forget to engage in conversation. It's like I've upped my binocular magnification, lucky enough to get a better view, but confounded by what to make of the new landscape. Me and Melanie and a purple flower in a vase.

We get the awkward, obvious stuff out of the way. The good-to-see-yous and the I'm-glad-you-could-make-its. I hold out my injured hand and tell her I tripped and sprained my pinky finger. My vulnerable state gives us both an advantage; we have something to laugh at together. I'm such a klutz! And then we're off.

"Your sister told me a lot about you," she offers.

I'm not sure this is a good start. "Hope it was good," I quip, and we laugh a little too long, and I want to say, No, really, I hope it was good, but I slurp at my ice water instead.

"She's a good egg, your sister. She cares about you."

"Yeah," I say, and start counting in my head the number of times Natalie refused my calls this week. More ice water.

"I've only known her a few months," she says and smiles. "But sometimes you can tell when you've met a good person."

"Yeah," I say, and think: I know exactly what you mean. I smile back. "I know exactly what you mean," I say. She looks at the flower and smiles again, a declaration of goodness: this is going well so far.

She tells me much more as the night goes on.

Some things verbally: she likes going out to movies instead of renting because she likes the smell of popcorn even though she doesn't eat any; she listens to classical music in the car, but sings out loud—poorly—when Guns N' Roses is on the radio; she loves to stare at the stars for hours, usually at predawn because this is when the earth is at its most still; she practices yoga during this silent time at Jasmine Beach, right before sunrise, every morning, no matter what is going on in the world. "The sun is so beautiful at dawn, Sid," she tells me. "You should see it sometime." I imagine the two of us sitting on the beach at sunrise, our eyes closed as the sun reveals its light and warmth. The two of us, breathing slowly and deliberately, holding our lotus position with great conviction, levitating above the Jasmine sand.

Other things she says nonverbally: laughing at my unfunny jokes, playing with her hair occasionally, smiling into the purple flower on the table as if it's the source of her good fortune to be enjoying herself so much, so unexpectedly.

Time moves faster than it should. A breezy, magical experience I'd forgotten about. And as I walk away from the café and Melanie walks in the opposite direction, I think about our inevitable second date, but I find myself unconsciously anticipating loud noises and mistakes, slipping and silences. "Let's do this again" plays over in my ears, but I'm also speculating if tonight is the night the stringy things attack my cerebral cortex. We will have dinner again soon, and while I can't wait, something inside me is fighting.

It doesn't help that, when I pull in my driveway, the door to the mailbox has been left open. That can only mean two things: someone took my mail or the mailman left it open. I can't imagine how either might happen. My trepidation deepens when I see what's inside—a single bright orange postcard with huge blue letters that read: COSTA RICA! I flip it over, and in that signature frilly penmanship it asks: "Do you know the way to San Jose?"

I shove it back in the mailbox, shut the door, and hold it closed. As if by pure determination I will make it disappear. I think of the inspirational posters on the walls of Wanderlust. *Create your own destiny! If you can conceive it, you can achieve it!* I take a deep breath and open the door again: still there. I snatch the postcard and slip it in my back pocket. I look around for witnesses, march straight inside the house, back to my bedroom, and kneel down beside the mattress. I pull out the box of postcards, toss in the latest, cover it back up, and push it back under. I lay down, exhausted.

I take a few more deep breaths to relax, like I learned on Cherry Hill. But what I'm trying to avoid comes anyway, as if by wishing it away I have actually wished it closer. Time pulls thin like saltwater taffy. Lilac candy fills the room with its sweet aroma, heady fluff spinning through the air like smiling faeries dancing in a sugarplum daydream until I fade away.

In my dreams, Melanie and I ride a Jet Ski over dark waters at night. It's cold. Lightning flashes in the distance. We're trying to reach land, but it's not visible.

I squeeze the throttle; Melanie squeezes me. Our Jet Ski slaps down hard on wave after wave; the icy sea-spray stings our faces. Growing numb from the plunging temperatures, I wonder if we'll make it.

Suddenly, our Jet Ski picks up speed, as if a weight has been lifted. We cruise over the water effortlessly and the horizon reveals itself. I turn back to tell Melanie we're almost home, but she's not behind me anymore. She's a hundred yards back, a speck in the sea.

I maneuver the bike around and head straight toward her, and that's when I see it: the dip in the level of the ocean, the circular pattern, a vortex of rushing water, and Melanie, swirling helpless in the clutches of a giant whirlpool.

I want to motor in and save her, but the Jet Ski will never make it out. I want to tell her there is no way I could have predicted this total nautical anomaly. I want to tell her how sorry I am, that it's all my fault. But I can only watch in horror as she rides the spiral downward.

We're here again, together, sitting in a restaurant across from one another. This time the flower between us is red, and it's not one but several—a bouquet of paper flowers, a harbinger of abundance. The Chinese Moon is not a place either of us has dined, but we've both heard good things about its authentic food. If the elaborate fan-folded napkins are any measure of quality, I'd say we're in for an exceptional culinary experience. A neon moon decorates the far wall, but it's unlighted. I mention this to Melanie. She tells me that according to her friend, the neon moon mimics the lunar cycle of the real moon, and because it's a new moon, it's kept dark.

"The new moon is when the Chinese New Year begins," she says. "It's good luck, I think. New beginnings and all that." She smiles and studies the menu.

The smells emanating from the kitchen tap into my main-line memories, and I begin to feel like I'm in Chinatown again, forever ago. Behind me, the kitchen doors swing open, followed by a barrage of authentic dialect. Rapid-fire vowels with hard edges sing through the dining room and cease just as suddenly when

the kitchen doors swing closed. Did someone say, *"Ning maa?"*
I go for the ice water.

Looking directly at Melanie puts me at ease. It's her hair, I
think: chocolate brown, no streaks of color, no blue or pink or
purple. I decide my best plan of action is to fully engage the conversation. If I'm talking, I'm not thinking. And, in fact, after we
order a pot of oolong tea, I find that I can't stop talking.

"Do you believe in old souls?" I ask.

"Oh I don't know. Souls, yes. Old and young ones? I
suppose."

"People often tell me I'm an old soul."

"Oh?"

"It's the strangest thing. I don't get it."

Melanie sips her tea. "Well I imagine that would be seen as a
compliment," she says, and smiles, and sips.

I play with the paper flowers. "These are nice," I say. "A nice
red. Or burgundy, maybe, or crimson."

"They're crimson."

"Crimson and clover," I say. "Over and over," I continue, and
then laugh. I feel like I'm blathering on like an idiot and say as
much, but she keeps assuring me she enjoys listening to me.

We both nod and sip and are quiet for a moment, but I have an
uncontrollable urge to talk about everything. I can feel it rising
in me like an unstoppable tide—a slow but steady surge of intimate details and boring stories and memories and—oh God no—
philosophies on life.

"I have a friend who believes you shouldn't say good-bye to
people," I say, "because that means you're saying good-bye to
their spirit."

And Melanie doesn't seem repelled by the comment; in
fact she seems to be ingesting it and thinking—not talking—about

this idea. But before she can share her thoughts, I'm on to another one.

"Some people believe if you're taken prematurely from life on Earth, you might hang around as a ghost until you get what you need to move on to the next life."

Melanie looks at me for a few seconds, considering this last declaration, and opens her mouth to respond, but I've got something else to say.

"Did you know that spirits often talk to mediums in symbols so the medium must not only make contact with the spirit but then translate the symbols to find meaning in the spirit's living counterpart?"

And,

"I used to think that the most exciting way to die was by avalanche."

And,

"Copper is the best choice for plumbing pipes due to the metal's durability and biostatic properties."

And,

"Fusiform cerebral aneurysms are not actually as dangerous as you might think."

And,

"Moor peat mud is rich in the clays and minerals known to reduce inflammation of the nerves and improve epidermal health."

And,

"There are over 25,000 objects in the sky above us right now floating in space."

And,

Dear God. I can't shut up.

I apologize for talking so much, but Melanie says she likes it when I talk, and brushes her hair out of her face. And I read once that if a girl plays with her hair when you're on a date, that means she's attracted to you. But the tide is reaching its high point, and who knows what else I might say to her. I excuse myself to the restroom.

Inside a stall, I brace my hands against the walls to maintain a standing position. I feel the tide ebbing, but not nearly as fast as I need it to ebb. The quiet of the restroom has given me a break from myself, but I can't believe all the things I've said. "Epidermal health?" I ask out loud to make sure I really said it. The question is full of reverb.

Maybe five minutes go by and I still feel full of words. Scenes and stories want out, to be told into existence, like dying stars gasping for their last light. But I can't scare this girl any more than I already have. I've spent weeks dreaming of coming to her rescue and now I'm here with the real Melanie and I'm drowning instead of helping. Maybe she's not the one who needs saving. I take a few deep, yogic breaths and walk back out to the dining room.

The lights have dimmed, indicating another level of evening—a deeper intimacy here at The Chinese Moon. Melanie isn't at our table. I look back to the restrooms in case she's taken a trip herself, but the waiter's expression explains it all: she's gone.

Her absence leaves me with a momentary sense of relief, the tide has completely ebbed now. But it's replaced by the stinking death of stranded sea life, and it makes me a little sick.

"What time is it?" I ask the waiter.

"Your date left five minutes ago, sir," he says. He tells me I've been gone over half an hour.

For a brief moment, I wonder if she's waiting for me on the

sidewalk outside, but she's better than that. I look at the red table flowers, which don't seem so abundant now that I've probably blown my last chance. What is wrong with me?

"How would you like to pay?" the waiter asks, and I reach for my credit card, knowing that it will never go through.

Driving clears my head—the movement, the white noise, the tangible feel of cause and effect as I push the gas pedal or brake. So I drive, and wait for clarity. I guess I should be feeling thankful that the restaurant owner happened to be one of Natalie's patients, and that Natalie was willing to cover my bill. I wouldn't have gotten off so easy, otherwise. I should also be feeling grateful that Melanie wasn't waiting outside the restaurant, ready to punch me in the stomach. But all I can think about is her eyes, how they smiled at me over dinner, how much of a good time we seemed to be having, and how I ruined it for both of us. It's especially difficult to feel thankful when my sister is yelling at me through my cell phone while I'm driving. But I'm pretty good at talking on the phone and driving at the same time, unlike some people. I put the phone on speaker and let it rest in my lap so I can drive with both hands. Natalie's voice pierces through the road noise.

"You just left her there?!"

"She left me."

"Because you vanished!"

"Just relax."

"You're telling *me* to relax?"

"Well, what do you want me to say?" I ask.

"How about 'I'm sorry' for starters?"

"I'm sorry."

"And then 'Thanks for paying for my dinner' would be good."

"I didn't know my card was maxed out."

"Jesus, Sid!"

"I don't know what to tell you."

"No kidding."

"Sorry and thank you," I say. I keep the wheel steady on the road, focus my stare on the highway.

"Well that's not really going to cut it, is it," she says.

"I'll pay you back, don't worry about it."

"I'm not worried about the fucking money, Sid!" Natalie is not the swearing type, so I know I've really upset her. She reserves this kind of language for when she's feeling helpless, or hopeless, and neither one is good. She seems to be feeling like this a lot more often since her pregnancy. And right now her voice sounds hoarse, desperate, as if she'd been screaming previous to our conversation. "I just don't understand how you could let this happen."

I let out a big sigh.

Natalie winds up again. "You know, I told her about Zoe and Mom. I told her about your past year, and she still wanted to meet you. So what the hell am I supposed to say about this?"

"I don't know what to tell you."

"I don't know what to tell you," she mocks, then says it again away from the receiver, to imaginary people she wants to have join in her resentment. "That's all you can come up with?"

I answer with silence, and continue my study of the road signs.

The Highway 20 overpass is three miles away, and I feel a sense of dread when I realize where I'm headed.

"Let me tell you something, Sid, because there's a lot I can tell."

"I bet."

"Let me tell you how it's been to be your sister for the past year."

"That'd be great, Nat."

"Let me tell you how it is to have thirty patients in my care daily, but the one who needs the most attention is my brother, who is perfectly healthy. My brother, who calls me five times a day, even though I tell him I can't talk, not because I don't want to but because I need to tend to people with *real physical ailments*."

"I won't ever call you again."

"Let me tell you about my brother, who tragically lost his girl-friend—"

"Here we go!"

"—but who doesn't know how to let go, over a year later."

My hands form a thin layer of sweat, greasing the steering wheel. I clamp down harder.

"A year," she says again, for maximum impact, "that's twelve months."

Still driving.

"He can't let go because he feels guilty that he somehow did something wrong, even though it was an accident. He can't let go because he doesn't want to admit that the relationship was over anyway."

Two miles to the Highway 20 overpass. "You don't know what you're talking about," I say. My mouth is dry. I feel something spark in my chest, a tiny ember burning a hole in my lung.

"You didn't love Zoe anymore, and you feel terrible about it."

I cough hard, or maybe it's a laugh. It's a loud noise, whatever it is.

"You didn't love her anymore, *Sid*."

I fucking hate it when she says my name like that. I punch the roof, but she keeps talking. The scar on my hand throbs.

"You two fought constantly. You were both done with each other, and then she died, and now you can't stand yourself, so you're screwing everything up as punishment—some kind of twisted atonement."

"That is fucking perfect, Nat. Sounds like you got me all figured out. I didn't realize you were a psychiatrist, too." The hot hole in my chest blossoms wider, threatens vital organs. "I just wish you'd be less subtle, you know, say what's really on your mind."

"You want me to be more direct?"

"Yeah, that'd be great!"

"I can definitely be more direct," she snarls. Her voice is muddy and distorted, like her mouth is pressed tight against the phone.

"Go for it," I say, and swallow hard against the heat rising in my neck.

"You got it!"

"Here we go!" I say, and then she goes.

"She wanted to travel, so you go to work at a travel agency."

"Really—"

"She wanted a dog, so you go buy a dog. Sound about right?"

"No," I say, because I want to tell her that's not how it happened with the dog.

"She died in that car accident and you lived," Nat says, "so you come up with reasons every day for why you should be dead too."

I want to challenge her on all of it, but my throat is smoldering and I can't speak. I notice the highway lines slipping by my car, one by one.

"Sid, you may have been in the hospital during Zoe's funeral, but she is deceased. She's gone. And it's a terrible, sad thing because it was an accident, but you are going to have to deal with this and move on because your life is not the only one affected by this." She's silent for a moment. I assume she's taking a deep breath to continue, but then I hear crying, which builds to sobbing. Suddenly she shouts: "God damn it!" Then more big, heavy, ugly sobs.

My throat constricts and my eyes get hot and weepy, and it's too much already. I roll the window down and toss out the phone. It skips along behind the car, tiny flashes of spinning light before it goes dark in the rearview mirror.

I feel like I've won and lost all at once, but I don't know what I've gained or given up. I punch the roof again. I yell to make a sound, to feel it in my throat. I shout at the road, at my sister, at everything. I punch the roof again. My hand hurts, but it helps somehow.

The chilly evening air pours in from the open window, howls through the cabin, cools my forehead, fills my lungs. The white highway divider lines continue to drift by the car; I can almost hear them as they slip past: dash, dash, dash. This deceitful rhythm synchronizes with the racing pulse in my hand as I approach the dark bend near the Highway 20 overpass, now only a quarter-mile away, according to the white reflective letters on the green highway sign.

I roll past the merging exits, and the rhythm doesn't stop abruptly or tragically, as it has before, because there are no other cars or trucks out tonight. No distracted drivers on their cell phones. No dog running across the highway. Not tonight. Instead, the rhythm gradually slows as I let up on the gas and pull over on the gravel shoulder.

I kill the lights.

It doesn't seem so bad here at night. Without a blazing sun illuminating the details, it's almost a peaceful place, like I'm not really here at the actual scene but just at any old highway along a grassy field in the middle of the night. It's weird how the world cleans up places, not people.

And now, with all signs of the crash gone, I can truly see it. That dog running across the highway. Every thought I had, every feeling. All the stupid things I was thinking. A dog ran into speeding traffic, in front of my car, and my first thought was that I hope we don't hit the dog because I don't want Zoe to wake up and be mad at me. She was napping so quiet next to me, if I could just get her home maybe we could have a few more minutes without arguing.

But then I noticed this dog's tongue drooping out of its mouth and I was thinking how the dog seemed out of its mind, like it was having a psychotic episode and that's why the dog ran into traffic in the first place. That's why it ran directly in front of our car. All of these things and my gamble was to keep on rolling because if I missed the dog, then we'd keep on rolling. The semi-trailer truck on Zoe's side didn't gamble my way. One of the last things I recall seeing was Zoe's seat belt snug against the door, not where it should have been, but left unfastened for comfort's sake. I felt our car lurch to the side, and then there was spinning and screeching and stopping.

I gained consciousness soon after, maybe one minute later, maybe five.

I saw the hole in the windshield. And next to me, the seat was empty. As if she'd flown away.

The whole world buzzed and my head and chest were killing

me, but I stared through the windshield, straight into the sun, for as long as I could, until it hurt, because I thought if I looked away, I'd lose her forever.

The dog sat outside my car. I pushed opened the door and he crept closer. He sat with me for a long time, licking my hand, until the paramedics arrived. Strange how this dog, so oblivious to having caused a major car accident, was so intuitive and knew I needed help. I remember telling him, "You have no clue," as the wreckage smoked around us, horns blared, and sirens wailed in the distance. "Absolutely zero," I told him. And we waited together for Zoe to come back down from the clouds.

I get out of my car and take a few wobbly steps. I try to fight this, but it's too big, there's too much to hide. There is no hole to crawl into here, no way to pretend this away. I'm on solid ground and it hurts like hell.

I lie down on the gravel roadside and stare up at the deep black night to find solace, but everything in me is breaking away. Every twisted memory and sweetened tragedy, all the bullshit lies and lost love and heartaches and panic attacks and phone calls. They are ripping their way out of me, bursting out in violent, moaning sobs and snot and tears, and wracking coughs.

I let it all go, knowing I need to say it, try to say it, and it seems ridiculous, because I know she can't hear me, but just fucking say it, Sid—*I'm sorry*. The words like pieces of glass in my throat.

Zoe would tell me not to worry, if she were here, she would say stop acting like an idiot and get back on your feet, and while you're at it, forgive yourself already. They call it an accident for a reason, and that's what this was—an accident. And she's right. And she's not here. It's just me. And after a while I'm just breathing. And I realize it's quiet again.

I am quiet again.

So I slowly stand up, walk over to my car, and get back in. I feel like I should call someone, but I'm not sure who anymore. I realize I've thrown my phone out the window, which is funny because I always promised Natalie I would do that someday. I don't turn my headlights back on because I like it that way, the night stretching on endlessly. I remember this is actually due to the lunar cycle, like Melanie talked about before I decided to run away like a coward.

A point of light catches my eye and floats silently across the sky—a satellite minding its path. I watch it for several seconds as it passes the Big Dipper and fades over the horizon. I journey home by the dark of the new moon.

As I pull in my driveway, I am exhausted. Opening the car door and walking up to the house feel like superhuman tasks. I'm not much of a drinker, but all I really want is some alcohol. I search the house, but there's no beer, no liquor, no wine.

Wait.

I trudge down the basement stairs. Under the dark green army blanket, there it is, the 1967 bottle of Bordeaux. "Sorry Mom," I announce and hold it up to the light. "Just going to make more room in there for you."

I rummage through the cupboards for a wine glass. If I'm going to drink forty-year-old wine, I might as well do it right. I find an old corkscrew hidden in the back of the silverware drawer. I peel back the foil and get to work on the cork; a steady pull releases the stopper, and with it the heady aroma of the decades-old wine. I pour it into the glass, watch the purple liquid with a cautious eye. No lilacs sprout forth, no clouds of flowers, no resentful spirits.

"You're free," I say to Mom, if she's even around, if she's even listening. "My turn," I say, and drink. It's fruity and bitter. I'm sure it's got hints of nut and vanilla and maybe even persimmon, but hell if I know. That's not really the point now. I swallow down the rest of the glass and pour another. I drink that too, and keep pouring.

I wonder if I was anywhere near Bordeaux when I visited Paris. I wonder if Zoe wanted to go there too, and if she knows how guilty I feel for having traveled so far. Me, stay-at-home Sid. I also wonder if Melanie will ever forgive me, and how many more glasses this bottle of wine will fill.

chapter

69

The smell of earth is all around me.
Slowly, I begin to realize it's because I am
in my backyard, or, more accurately, under
it. I frown into the noon sun. My face muscles
aren't working right; they're sluggish, like I'm covered in an alien
film. I attempt to open my mouth, but my skin is taut. Caked-on
dirt crumbles away.

I fight my way to a sitting position, get nose-to-nose with the
lawn's edge. I try to remember what happened that would put me
here. My headache and dry mouth tell me wine was involved. I
remember things, but they're foggy—vague notions of people
and ghosts, of memories. I climb back up to the surface and head
inside, where my answering machine blinks with the number
four. Four more than I'm used to. Somehow these unheard messages worry me more than the mystery of last night's activities.

I push the play button. A robot woman's voice says: "Message one."

"Sid. Pick up. It's your sister. Pick up the phone."

Beep. "Message two."

"Sid! Answer the phone. I know you're there. Hello?"

Beep. "Message three."

"Sid, I'm going to keep calling you and leaving messages until you pick up the damn phone."

Beep. Robot woman says: "Message four."

"Okay, you know what? No I'm not. This is my message, so pay attention. I'm sorry for what I said last night. I just thought maybe I could shock you out of whatever you're going through. But it was totally callous. I would be a terrible psychiatrist. I don't know what you're going through. I'm such a bitch, I don't know what's wrong with me. I'm pregnant, okay? It's the hormones. It's no excuse, but if you want to know true suffering, get yourself pregnant." She laughs a little, then drops her voice a notch. "Okay, that was a joke. I'm also a bad comedian. I'm a terrible matchmaker too. Forget about Melanie."

"No, that's not—" I say to the answering machine, but she keeps going.

"Do what you gotta do. I'll think of something to tell her. Just call me back, okay? Please?"

After a long pause, I hear sniffles in the background.

"Please," she says finally, "I'm so sorry. Call me back."

Beep.

The robot lady says: "You have no more new messages."

My head starts to pound, and I'm sure there's a tumor at the root of it, but I'm guessing it's nothing any trip in the giant humming machine will cure. Instead, I go to my bedroom and pull out the box of postcards. I carry them to the garage, grab the shovel, walk to the edge of the hole I just climbed out of, and drop them in.

With each throb of my temples, I throw a spadeful of dirt from the mound. I watch the box disappear beneath tosses of earth. I listen to the sounds of digging. *Shk—thump—shk.* One by one. For what seems like hours, I watch the hole fill in, hoping Gerald won't see me across the yards and offer his help. Eventually the hole becomes level with the yard, and I'm back on even ground.

I drop the shovel and walk back in the house, to the bathroom. I strip, step into the shower, and turn the water on full blast. Mud spirals down the drain in tiny rivers of black, but I don't feel any cleaner. I lather up with my bar of spicy green soap, but I do not feel invigorated like the commercials have assured me I would. I dry off, get dressed, and lie down to take a nap. When I wake, out of habit, I go to the mailbox.

I walk slowly across the lawn in my bare feet and can feel every blade of grass, the ants crawling over my toes. A breeze blows across my face, tosses my hair, cools my neck; I inhale the sweet smell of honeysuckle and pine from the neighbors' yards. All my senses come together, so clear, like this whole past year has come to this moment, to the mailbox, today, because something inside needs to be seen. Something for me.

Mary Jo stands in her yard, her armpit resting firmly on her mailbox. She is not her jovial self. She frowns at the bright sun, and does not brush her hair away when the wind blows it in her eyes. She shakes her head at me, as if she knows what I'm up to, and doesn't like it.

When I open my mailbox, it appears empty, but the sun is casting a strong shadow, so it's hard to tell. I glare at Mary Jo accusingly. Her squinty eyes widen, then narrow again. We study each other for a moment, eyes locked across the asphalt rift of the suburban street. I turn to the mailbox. It seems darker and deeper than its bread-loaf dimensions, like a whole life could be hidden away in there, lost and forgotten. I'm tempted to reach inside but I clap it shut and walk away.

There is a Zen-like state achieved through having a clean work space. Unburdened by clutter, my chi flows freely throughout my Wanderlust cubicle. The walls are bare but for the Costa Rica postcard, which I've tacked up directly in front of me. I feel an even deeper sense of tranquility because I know what I'm going to do today. As a result of my decision, I feel bad for Steve and the world of travel-package salespeople, but they will keep going. The Randomizer will keep dialing.

I haven't called Natalie back, but I will soon. She's probably waiting for my apology-acceptance call, but I don't know what to say yet. I wonder if she called Melanie and told her to forget about that crazy brother of hers. Maybe Melanie has already forgotten me. I hope not. I don't have the energy to think about it all, and I've got calls to make.

Steve walks toward my cubicle and nods a greeting. His eyes sweep over my work space. He grimaces, and a little dimple forms in his left cheek: the dent of disappointment. He prefers a lot of color on employees' walls. He likes to see photos and posters and calendars and sales charts—clear evidence of seller motivation, that his salespeople believe in the product. He continues his walk down the hall, smiling at the other staff and their vibrant walls.

But I remain pleased with the symmetry and simplicity of my single postcard against the space of the cubicle. All edges are equidistant from the sides of the wall, as if the wall itself were created to frame this very postcard.

I make a few calls, waiting for the right one. I reel out my pitch and people hang up on me. Some folks say it sounds great but they can't afford a vacation right now. Another call, another hang-up. This happens several times, as it always does, brief digital rejections to my fiber-optic ego. Then I sell a Caribbean honeymoon package to a guy my age who thinks it will be a wonderful surprise for his fiancée. It's a nice victory for both of us, a good note to end on, but it's not the call I'm looking for. I'll know it when it feels right.

I watch The Randomizer do its thing one more time, and after four rings a young kid answers. The computer screen says I've called Tom Winfred.

"Hello, is this Tom Winfred?" I ask the boy.

"No," he says.

Video game guns explode in the background.

"Is he going to be home soon?"

The boy pauses. "No," he says, more serious.

"Well when would be a good time to reach him?"

The video game guns quit firing.

"He's not here," the boy says.

"Do you know when he'll be back?" I ask.

"He's not coming back."

"Oh," I muster. A few seconds drag by.

Steve's voice whispers in my head. The omniscient supervisor has arrived. "Ask for his mother. Get the kid off the phone."

"I'm really sorry, buddy," I say. "We won't bother you again, okay?"

"Ask for his mother, Sid. Don't talk to the kids."

The boy makes a muffled sound. "My dad left six months ago. My mom says to take us off the list."

"You've got a good mom there. You'll be all right. Sorry for ruining your video game. Did you win?"

"No. You can't win this game. It's not like that."

"Well keep practicing. You'll get there."

Steve pipes in with his baseball announcer voice, which means he's quickly encroaching. "What are you doing-oing? Don't talk to the kids-ids. Next call-all."

"Hey kid, you've got a lot to look forward to," I say, and wish him good luck. The call is over, and The Randomizer starts dialing another one.

Steve stands directly behind me. I can smell his disapproval.

"Sid, seriously. What was that?"

"We'll get him next time," I say, and give him the thumbs-up.

He's a little confused with my positive outlook, but nods and keeps walking. He rounds the corner, out of sight.

I pull my earpiece out and place it on Bug-Out Bob. On a yellow sticky note I write, "Steve: Good luck with the beaucoup bucks. Thanks for the opportunity. Best, Sid."

I roll my chair under the desk and tack my note on the wall below the Costa Rica Paradise postcard. I take one last look at the lush fauna and tropical toucans, wave good-bye to the happy couple running on the beach, and make my way to the nearest exit.

Outside, the air is fresh and clean. I take a deep breath and it is invigorating. I feel like I could run a million miles of seashore today, or travel somewhere new and undiscovered. I feel lighter than usual, like I could fly.

That night I dream of beaches. Tropical landscapes with coconuts and hammocks. Swaying trees and ukulele music. Cold, icy drinks with crimson umbrellas. Highball glasses sweating on teak furniture. Fire pits and sugar sand. Warm ocean breezes. The lush rhythm of the surf as the waves unfurl and melt into the shore. Like breathing. Like paradise.

I awaken with a startle and sit bolt upright in bed. In the waking world, I feel sick. The sudden movement upward has left me dizzy and disoriented in the darkness of my own bedroom.

"Beach," I say out loud. My eyes adjust and I look over at the soft, red-digit glow of my digital clock. It's 4:30 a.m. A cruel hour to be awake. "I need to go to the beach," I tell myself, and force my body to its feet.

The airline business should call red-eye flights dark-purple. My eyes actually feel bruised from being up and open so early.

And when I pull my car into the Jasmine Beach parking lot, the blues and violets of the night sky shine their way through as well. The sun will be up soon, which means I don't have much time.

The beach is incredibly quiet, as if the sand has absorbed all the sound. The gulls haven't begun calling yet, and traffic is eerily absent. Only the hush of waves. The wide strip before me is lumpy and dark, not quite discernible from the black water in the near distance. I stumble over little dunes, search the shoreline for familiar figures. My hands are shaky. This is not paradise, this is not like breathing.

The stars begin to vanish with dawn's arrival, which I've always found a bit sad, but the hope of something brighter lurks beneath the horizon. I see a woman doing yoga a few dozen yards away. She has tied herself up in a pretzel position, but appears peaceful despite her interweaving limbs. I make my way toward her, push my reluctant feet through shifty ground.

When I arrive next to her, she opens her eyes to take me in

peripherally, then shuts them again. She doesn't seem alarmed that a stranger on a public beach has come to join her meditation. She must know it's me. I plop down a few feet away in case I'm wrong, and stare out at the dark, vast lake. I watch the last star fade into the growing turquoise of the sky, and I wish we could sit here together, silently, until it's dawn again tomorrow. I muster up the courage to break the silence.

"Melanie," I say, "I want you to know something."

She stares straight ahead. She hasn't run away or attacked me, so that's good. I stare straight ahead too, and talk to the lake, hoping it will serve as a good mediator.

"I'm sorry for leaving you the other night. I mean, really sorry. With-deep-feelings-of-regret kind of sorry." She holds her gaze, a petrified oak tree. "I can't really explain it," I say. The waves lap rhythmically. One by one. Lap, lap, lap.

She waits for more.

I sit up and try to mimic her yoga position, but my limbs don't bend like hers. I try to fold my right leg under my left knee, but it hurts to have my limbs at such odd angles. I'm not very good at bending. I give up and lay my hands on my lap instead, hold my legs straight out. This is hard enough. I take a deep breath.

"I really enjoy your company," I say. "I feel like we connect somehow, like we're on the same frequency or something, so I don't know why—this all sounds so ridiculous. It's just—"

I shut my eyes tight and watch the ghost image of the sunrise on the back of my eyelids—a blue-and-orange flashing apparition. I can't look directly at it or it moves away, floating slowly off to the left, outside my field of vision. I need to say something concrete here, something that puts this all into perspective, or I will lose her. But all I can do is think of everything all at once.

I think about my dad and his copper pipes. I think about

Natalie and the quickness with which she made a baby after Mom died. Dr. Singh with his plaques, Gerald with his underground library. Candyce's dream interpretations. Mom's wine bottle. Zoe's postcards. Everybody trying so hard to be remembered, to stay connected to everyone else. There's only one way I can think to explain all these thoughts to Melanie, and it will sound like madness.

"My dead mother's spirit lived in a bottle of 1967 Bordeaux," I say.

The sun shoots a knife of light into my tired eyes. I try to adjust my position but my legs are full of needles, the sand beneath me an indifferent mass of cold granules. I sit up awkwardly and wait for the inevitable.

Melanie pushes out a long, deep breath. "Well," she says, and makes me wait—a long wait, the kind that makes you wonder if words were actually spoken, or if you just thought they were. "That's pretty dramatic," she says. "I don't know if I'm up for so much drama."

"I understand," I say, a little relieved. "I'm not really either."

And I realize this is it, the end of all my daydreams and rescue fantasies, the last moments of a promising relationship that never quite got off the ground. But then she tilts her head from side to side, as if the options she's weighing are a physical presence inside her skull. I imagine tiny colored balls bouncing around the interior of her cranium, like a circus game, and I wonder which one will drop out of her ear to be the winner. She makes a humming noise, which I'm happy to hear because I know she's working on an answer, but I can't stand this.

Finally, after so much silence, she speaks. "I do love Bordeaux," she says, with a welcoming but unfinished tone, like maybe she wants me to help her along a little.

Just then, a streak of light blazes across the horizon—a shooting star burning out. I wonder if Satellite Sixty has just fallen from the sky, destroying residences or setting cities on fire. Or maybe only I witnessed its descent, a silent dissolve into the water, unnoticed by the rest of humanity. Forgotten. But soon I realize that the world has not ended. In fact, I can feel it underneath me, albeit cold and wet and fairly uncomfortable.

In my peripheral vision, Melanie has extended an open hand. I don't look at the hand directly because I don't want it to go away. Instead I stare forward at the sun as it pokes its orange round head over the horizon. I feel a certainty that the sun is amused by me, that maybe it's even laughing at everyone. Because to the sun, there is no rising and setting, only watching us spin around in circles. I suddenly have a strong affinity for it. I forgive it for all its brightness and burning, for all the pain it's caused.

The wet sand has soaked through my pants—a cold, unpleasant sensation. I adjust my position by pushing off the ground, but it only rides my pants up further. My hands are dirty now, my clothing ruined.

Melanie's hand is still extended. Her fingers wiggle at me, waiting for my response. And while we're far from being orbs of lotus light floating above Jasmine Beach, I think I finally know what to do.

I reach out to get a better hold.

acknowledgments

I would like to say thanks to Harper Perennial, and especially my editor, Carl Lennertz, for his wonderful insight, keen eye, abundant generosity, and exclamation points.

Thanks to my amazing agent, Sandra Bond, for her guidance, hard work, and enthusiasm. Most important, for believing in my manuscript, and getting it in the right hands.

In Milwaukee, *Postcards* spent countless Wednesday evenings at the Redbird Studio roundtable workshops. Thank you, Judy Bridges, for creating such a great atmosphere for writers. And thanks to everyone at Redbird for the feedback, encouragement, and camaraderie.

Special thanks to those who took the time and energy to read my first draft in its ugly entirety: Andy Jurkwoski, Dave & Mary Jo Thome, Les Huisman, Kari Barnes, and Kelly Schroeder. Your initial feedback was incredibly helpful.

Also a big thank-you to everyone at Pikes Peak Writers, for your support and excellent writing resources.

Thanks to my brutha, Andy, for celebrating and commiserating over writing, drinking beer, and bringing the metal. To my good friend, Chuck Freund, thanks for all the caffeine, and talking books, and for introducing me to a really groovy girl. And to Paul Block, thanks for answering the phone.

To my family: Keith & Diane Farber, Kari & Dan & Nina Barnes, John & LaVon Schroeder, Jill & Juan & Lukie & Logan Valdez. Thanks for your unconditional love and support. Family is everything. Thank you for everything.

To my late mother, Kathleen, thanks for your sense of humor and the red hair.

Most especially, thanks to my wonderful and beautiful wife, Kelly, for your unwavering belief in me, for continuing to encourage my crazy dreams, and generally keeping me happy, healthy, and laughing.

About the author

About the book

Insights,
Interviews
& More...

Read on

Meet Kirk Farber

Where were you born?

I was born and raised in Oconomowoc,
Wisconsin. 1971.

My dad was a textbook salesman, and my
mom was the Avon lady. My dad would go on
trips for a week at a time and come back with
stories of his travels and presentations. We
always had books piled around the house
because of his job. I'm sure some of my
storytelling comes from him. My mom was a
homemaker but also a saleswoman, so she was
very active in the community, very connected
with people. I think I got my sense of humor
from her, as well as the red hair. My sister, Kari,
also has the red hair. The three of us were quite
the spectacle growing up.

When did you first start writing?

I was a hyper kid, so I didn't write my first novel
when I was five years old or anything like that.

My parents directed my energy into playing the drums, so I spent most of my youth playing music and wanting to be a rock drummer. I eventually ended up playing in a band throughout my twenties, but as a kid, I didn't really seek out books much. When I did, it was the Chronicles of Narnia, and the Douglas Adams books, and Ray Bradbury. I enjoyed weird stories, surreal stories, funny stories. Still do.

Writing really started for me in high school. I took an advanced composition class and strangely enjoyed all of the assignments. It was a class that many people feared and loathed, but I had fun with it, which was exactly the opposite of my math class experience.

One of my high school teachers, Mrs. Newburg, was very passionate about literature and taught in unconventional ways that really made books fascinating. When we read *Lord of the Flies,* she had the class chant "Deus ex machina!" over and over like savages. And after we read *Welcome to the Monkey House,* she took us to see Kurt Vonnegut speak at a local university, which was a thrill. His stories and books made a huge impression.

One big turning point for my writing came at the beginning of my freshman year in college. My mother died from cancer a few weeks into the school year. I took a couple of weeks off to be with family, and when I returned, I just sort of isolated myself for a while. I remember going to the university bookstore and seeing all of the assigned novels for various literature classes, and I felt compelled to read all of them. I bought fifteen or twenty novels and spent most of my first semester reading. I read *Slaughterhouse-Five, The Catcher in the Rye, Catch-22*—all the stuff you'd expect on the freshman college list. But I had never spent so much time reading, and suddenly there were all of these incredible worlds to visit, all these stories that needed to be read and new ideas that needed to be written down. And that was it. I got the bug and have never stopped.

Any odd jobs to support your writing?

I've worked as a catastrophe cleaner, a caregiver, a group home supervisor, a rock drummer, and a website programmer.

Currently I work at a library, which is a great day job for a writer because you are surrounded by books and people who love books. Your coworkers also happen to be very savvy at finding information, which can be helpful for research. My job is in interlibrary loan, so I process the books our patrons want but we don't happen to own in our huge collection. So I get to see some very specific, unusual stuff come through, which can be great for story ideas or just personal entertainment. *1978 Collectible Salt & Pepper Shaker Pricing Guide*? Check. *Mind Control for Your Slaves During the Coming Apocalypse*? Check. *Electromagnetic Subterfuge Experiments with Reverse Angled Matrix Pressure Static Gages*? All three volumes, please. ᕦ

A Conversation with Kirk Farber

So, a book about postcards from a dead girl? What was your inspiration?

My initial inspiration came from a song called "Letters from the Dead" by a Nashville band called The Silver Seas (formerly The Bees). The lyrics are about someone who has found postcards from a past relationship and he doesn't know what to do with them. I was always listening to their whole album, and every time that song came up, my "what if" question would resurface: What if instead of discovering old postcards, they were being sent to you, but you weren't sure if the sender was alive or dead?

One day I sat down to write the first scene of the book (where Sid receives a postcard and suffers the accompanying anxiety-and-lilac spell), and two more scenes immediately followed that same day. The themes of the book naturally developed from there. I didn't set out to write a book about this or that. I just had this main conflict, this character in crisis. But as I wrote, I started exploring things like memory and idealization of the past. And disconnection, especially with language. Sid is always misunderstanding what people say, or hearing them wrong, or not hearing them at all. Often his dog is the only one who understands him.

I was also interested in how we deal with loss and tragedy—how we can put too much emphasis on escaping, or try too hard to be happy when maybe we just need to feel miserable for a while. Most of the people in the story get along just fine in life, yet Sid can't stop flailing. I found a lot of humor in Sid's flailing, though, because we've all done it—hit the brick wall a dozen times before we learn we're actually supposed to go around it. I figure if you can't laugh at some of the inevitable suffering in life, you might lose your mind.

What was your writing process for this novel?

I knew the beginning and the end before I really got going, so I just had to fill in all that middle part, which took about two years. I started by writing longhand, basically brainstorming, filling up legal pads with thoughts and themes until scenes started to reveal themselves. During that time I wrote up 3x5 index cards with the guts of the scenes. Then I hung a bunch of cork on my wall and tacked all the cards up so I could see the whole book. I liked to see all the story points and character arcs, so I'd have these cards and charts and scribbles all posted on my wall. After a while, my office got to looking like that Russell Crowe movie about the guy with schizophrenia.

A huge part of writing the novel was the rewriting, which I did with the help of my roundtable group at Redbird Studio in Milwaukee. We met every other week for read-alouds and critiques, and their feedback was invaluable. Plus the sense of community really made the lonely part of writing much more tolerable, and the regular sessions motivated me to keep pumping out scenes. If you can find a writing community who are honest and supportive, I highly recommend it. Just knowing other people are "out there" doing this writing thing can be worth your time and the price of admission. Honest, constructive feedback is priceless. Now that I live in Colorado, I'm part of Pikes Peak Writers, which is a great big group that is very active and connected—there is always something going on with PPW.

Do you have any writing rituals?

I tend to write when the world is quiet. Late night is best. I need total silence to hear myself think, and I achieve this by wearing foam earplugs as well as a set of noise reduction earmuffs. I look kind of ridiculous with this gear, but it gets the job done. I can't listen to music while I'm writing because I'll focus on the melody or instruments or lyrics. I'm pretty much a caveman: if I try to do more than one thing at a time, I get frustrated and confused and start grunting at the fireball in the sky.

If the writing isn't going well, I try to remind myself that as long as I sit at my desk long enough, something will get written. One sentence, even. It's kind of a trick for me. Just write one sentence for today, Kirk. And then inevitably more will follow. But if I sit down to write 1,200 words, it's a struggle.

The coolest thing about writing for me is the metaphysical part of it, how one minute you can be staring at a blank piece of paper, and the next you're off in your imagination, or the ether, or whatever you call it, and an hour later there is a page or a scene written down that didn't exist before. Norman Mailer called writing "the spooky art," and I agree.

How did Postcards *find a publisher?*

It started with my receiving a phone call on my birthday from literary agent Sandra Bond saying she wanted to sell my manuscript, which was a really great birthday present. After I signed with her in March, I settled in for the big wait of her sending the manuscript out to houses. I assumed it would take six to eight months because publishing is a very slow-moving machine. And I was preparing myself for the inevitable rejections, having gone through that process with short fiction.

But about one month later, Sandra called to let me know someone at HarperCollins was very interested, in fact was already faxing her pages of edits. This person was the estimable Carl Lennertz. He loved what he'd read but had some improvements in mind, so Carl and I worked on editing the book over the summer and fall. After several drafts and passing the muster of several more readers, Harper Perennial made an offer on Election Day. Quite a wonderful day, that one. ◡

Author's Picks

These novels have always stuck with me and really sparked my "you should write a novel" impulses:

Slaughterhouse-Five: Kurt Vonnegut is one of those writers who totally engages my imagination. Science fiction and literary thriller and satire all wrapped up in one bizarre, beautiful book. This is one of my favorites, as well as his short story collection, *Welcome to the Monkey House.*

Fight Club: Chuck Palahniuk's style knocked me out (ooh, bad pun)—sparse, provocative, and original. So much going on in this book, such a great twist at the end.

The Beach: Another summer book that swept me away. Alex Garland's take on *Lord of the Flies* was all-consuming for me. This updated paradise-gone-wrong story was totally engrossing.

Misery: This was the first book I remember not being able to put down. In fact, my boss at my summer job caught me carrying it in my back pocket and yelled at me. I just couldn't stop reading. Other books I love by Stephen King are *The Shining* and *The Dark Half* and *Bag of Bones*—hmm, all books about writers in peril.

A Trip to the Stars: Nicholas Christopher made me stop reading books for a month after I finished this story about a young boy named Enzo who is separated from his family when he's kidnapped at a planetarium. Intricate and heartfelt as Enzo searches for the people he's lost in his life. You also learn about mysticism, spiders, vampires, celestial navigation, and botany along the way.

The Virgin Suicides: What a beautiful book. Dark, lyrical, poignant. All good things, from Jeffrey Eugenides. Love this book.

Author's Picks *(continued)*

The Great Gatsby: This is my "classics" pick. I reread this recently after fifteen years and just loved it. I think this Fitzgerald guy has got a future in writing.

In the Lake of the Woods: Haunting, dreamy, and tragic. A love story and a horror story at the same time. A gracefully written thriller. Tim O'Brien is one of my favorite authors. I think of this book every time I water the plants.

Other writers who do the dreamy, surreal, literary thing I love so much are Paul Auster and Haruki Murakami. I get sucked in to their stories, and it's like a magic trick: I try to figure out how they got me to the end and I can't, but I'm happy to be there. ∽

Don't miss the next book by your favorite author. Sign up now for AuthorTracker by visiting www.AuthorTracker.com.